W9-BND-781

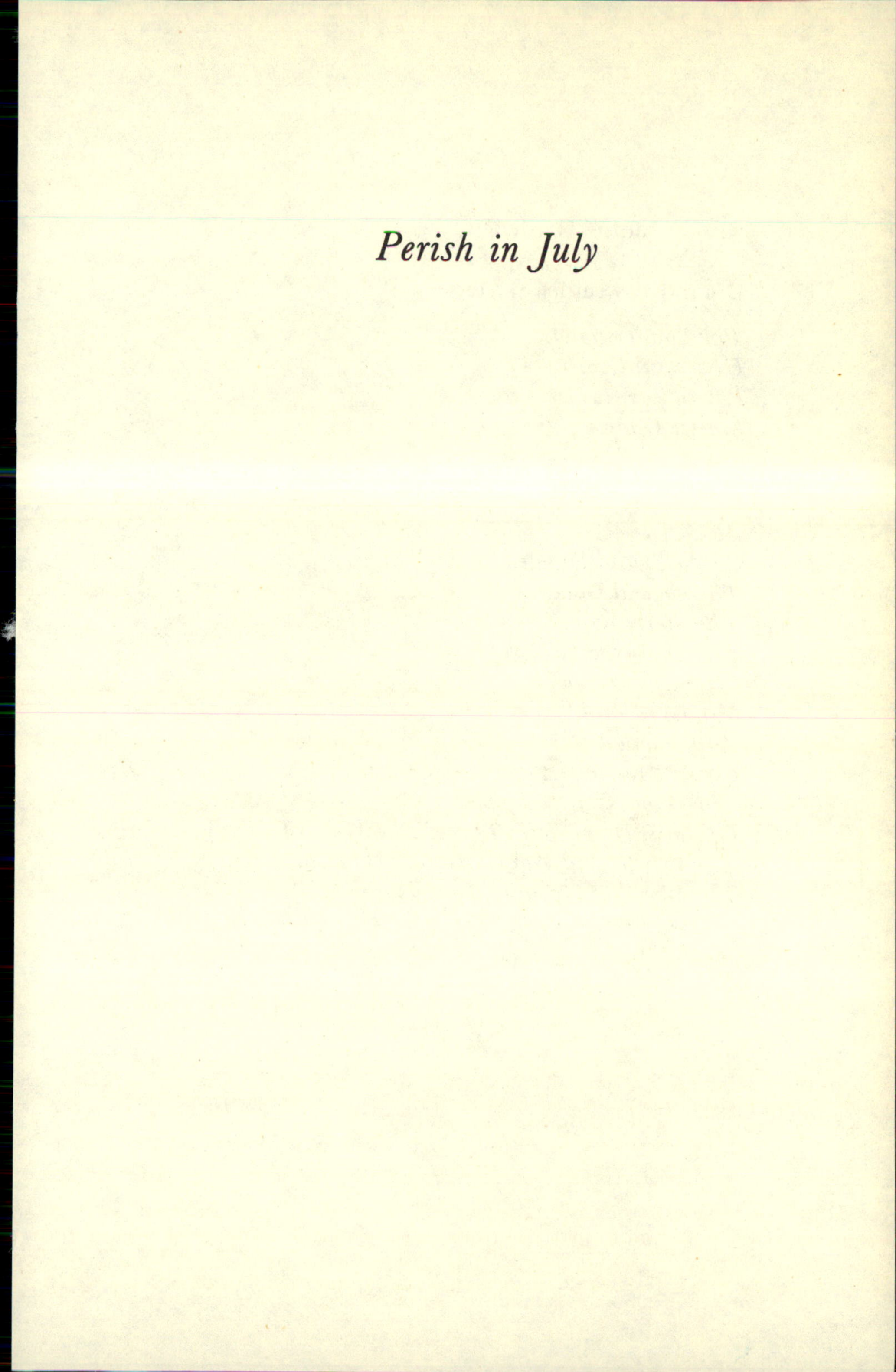

Perish in July

Also by Mollie Hardwick:

Doran Fairweather Mysteries

The Bandersnatch
Uneaseful Death
Parson's Pleasure
Malice Domestic

Historical Novels

Blood Royal
By the Sword Divided
The Crystal Dove
The Merrymaid
The Shakespeare Girl
I Remember Love
Monday's Child
Willowwood
Lovers Meeting
The Duchess of Duke Street
Upstairs, Downstairs Three: The Years of Change
The War to End War (Upstairs, Downstairs)
The World of Upstairs, Downstairs

PERISH IN JULY

Mollie Hardwick

St. Martin's Press
New York

 For information, address St. Martin's Press, 175 Fifth Avenue, New York, N.Y. 10010.

Library of Congress Cataloging-in-Publication Data

Hardwick, Mollie.
Perish in July / Mollie Hardwick.
p. cm.
ISBN 0-312-04402-X
I. Title.
PR6058.A6732P47 1990
823'.914—dc20

89-77956
CIP

First published in Great Britain by Century Hutchinson Ltd.

First U.S. Edition
10 9 8 7 6 5 4 3 2 1

1

To pick up some silver

Doran and Rodney Chelmarsh walked, hand in hand, through the lych-gate of St Crispin's Church, Abbotsbourne. A lot of villagers had attended the service, more out of respect for their ex-vicar, Rodney, than affection for the girl whose ashes had just been given burial.

Helena Chelmarsh, Rodney's crippled daughter by his first wife, had been what kindly people called difficult. Her tantrums and bouts of hysteria-induced illness, brought on by her obsessive dependence on her widowed father, had effectively kept him from marrying the girl he loved, Doran Fairweather, the young antique dealer.

Until five years ago. Since their marriage Helena had been sent to day school and had become a reformed character – almost. Christopher, Doran's son, known as Kit, now four years old, had become the focus of Helena's life until a sudden late spring chill had struck her down and killed her within two days.

No more driving her to school and collecting her in her folding invalid chair. No more fear of what it would be like if her progressive disease took her over altogether. No more Helena.

The local mourners stayed well behind, leaving the Chelmarshes to make their way back to Bell House, the pretty Queen Anne house which had been Doran's home before her marriage. It was kinder not to talk to the Reverend – as he still was, since the church authorities had kindly forgiven his resignation from St Crispin's on the grounds that he could no longer tolerate having to use the new Prayer Book and Bible. Instead he was allowed to act as vicar-in-charge of St Leonard's at Elvesham, a hamlet up on the Downs, where the congregation was small but active.

Doran saw with pity and intense love the increase of grey in Rodney's brown hair, still thick and crisp at forty-three. Her own delicate prettiness had not gone untouched by the work and worry.

'I wish I'd been nicer to her,' she said. 'They say one always does. But somehow in Helena's case it was worse. Even when she got more . . . easier. I didn't handle it properly. I did love her, you know. Only not enough.'

Rodney took off his heavy-rimmed spectacles, wiped them, and gave her his peculiarly sweet smile, which had wrought havoc in the hearts of several impressionable females in his congregation.

'None of us ever loves enough. If we did, we wouldn't be human. But I know how you tried, and what you did. And you gave her Kit – that was the most important thing anyone ever did for her. And now it's over. We have to get on with our lives, and try not to let Kit miss her too much.'

Doran took in a deep breath of the damp air, held it, and let it go. The old, old routine exercise for temper or tension or abysmal lowness of spirit. She could well understand why some people got roaring drunk after a funeral, though to a less degree why they found comfort in tea parties with sandwiches and cold ham. But to go home and open the scotch would do no good to anyone, least of all Helena.

'That's right,' she said. 'It's been about the most awful morning of our lives. I know you've taken thousands of funerals, well, hundreds, but never one like this. Poor you. Poor all of us. But it's over now. So –

like you said, we carry on. And you'll go over to Radio Dela tomorrow as arranged.'

Rodney looked startled. 'Will I?'

'Naturally. You can't go back on the new project. It's extremely important, recording the memories of old people while they're still with us, and using them for a parish history. There won't be many of them left if you don't get on with it.'

'True. True. Mr Beamish.'

'That's right. Mr Beamish. And don't forget to take your recording gear, and your camera. Don't ramble on too much, let him do the talking.'

They were approaching their own gate.

'Look.' Doran pointed to the neighbouring garden. 'The magnolia flowers are falling. Must be the damp spring.' The damp spring which had laid Helena under another flowering tree, the late cherry in the churchyard. 'Come in quick,' she added, 'or Perfect Paula will get you.'

The Bergs were no longer next-door neighbours, the exotic Cosmo and Richenda, whose designs on Doran and Rodney had been persistent but unsuccessful. What a pity they'd gone, taking with them an element of excitement. There was something stimulating in the thought that if one allowed oneself to be lured into the next-door neighbours' for an innocent gin and tonic, it might end in a fate considerably more agreeable than death, though it never had.

Vi Small, Doran's domestic help, shook the crumbs from a tablecloth at the kitchen door.

'She's at it again, I see,' she observed to Doran, who was hand-washing one of Kit's garments. 'Sweeping up the petals.' There was no need to ask who.

'Wearing green wellies, an apron with a big pocket for trowels and shears and things, proper gardening gloves and not a hair out of place?'

'That's right. Well, she always does, doesn't she, Mrs French? Not a one for letting people see her in a mess.'

'Nor is she,' said Doran grimly. 'I try, Heaven knows I try, with a rampant child who can be relied on to be where he shouldn't, and a husband coming home at all hours, I really work at it, yet I finish up looking like something nasty from one of those old kitchen sink plays.'

Vi surveyed her employer with calm detachment. She admired, with reservations, the efficient Mrs Paula French though she wouldn't have exchanged Miss Doran for her. (Not Miss Doran any more, of course, though it still said Fairweather Antiques over the Eastgate shop.)

'I shouldn't worry, if I was you. Nobody'd ever think you was turned thirty.'

'Thanks.'

Vi noted the sharp tone, and tactfully changed the subject. She was herself conscious of the passing of time, but what was half a century, after all? Just figures on paper, not the way you looked or felt. She straightened her back, remembering the figures of Roman goddesses Miss Doran had compared her to. No need to let domestic work spoil the figure. Every Friday evening her hair received a discreet application of a home shampoo guaranteed to keep it darkly glossy.

'What's Mr Rodney up to today, then?'

'Oh, he's gone somewhere for Radio Dela – some village in Thanet. Taken Kit with him, thank Heaven.'

'That's why the house is so quiet, is it?'

'It is,' said Doran fervently. 'And that's why I'm off to Eastgate as soon as I've finished throwing this recipe together. Black olives? Why do they say black olives? They look like little rubber footballs and I should think they'd spoil the taste of the meat.'

'Why don't you let me finish it, and get off nice and early?'

'Oh, Vi, would you? You're a natural-born angel. It's just that I feel rotten about not concentrating on special cooking, but when I follow these recipes they never seem to come out looking like the picture in the book, and I saw Kit making a pile of the last one at the side of his plate. For the poor birds, he said. Strictly for the birds, that's me. Here you are.'

She propped up the grease-marked volume and thankfully washed the onion-choppings off her hands.

'Her next door's a cordon bleu cook,' Vi said.

'She is. She would be. The only time we went to dinner there it was four-star stuff, all done without the faintest sign of effort in the kitchen and guaranteed to make one feel that she *knew* all we eat here is shop hamburgers and chips.'

'But you don't, Miss Doran.'

'I know, I know. I'm only being bitchy, Vi, some people do that to me and Perfect Peerless Paula's one of 'em.'

Vi heard her whistling, slightly off-key, as she ran upstairs. Shaking her head, she gave her attention to the preparation of the dish. By the time she had exercised her skills on it the poor birds were going to be out of luck.

Rodney let the car go its own way across the bridge which was taking him and Kit from Kent into the Island of Sheppey. His spirits rose at being in what was almost a tiny foreign country, away from familiar scenes and places. He was on a less than exciting mission: the seeking out of a local antiquary, whom rumour reported to be very deaf and extremely querulous.

'But it makes a change, doesn't it, Kit? From all those old churches we used to go to?'

Kit looked up, gave his father a beaming smile, and

returned to his current preoccupation, a little plastic box containing miniature goal-posts and a miniature football, the aim being to get the ball into the goal, though it had been fiendishly designed to go almost anywhere else. In fact, Kit had been rather too young to be taken on many of Rodney's journeys to interesting Kent churches, for the benefit of Radio Dela, and as a cleric Rodney didn't believe in forcing too much church on his son. When they grew up they were all too likely to head quite the other way.

Now Dela was sending him out to discover interesting characters, people old enough to remember the past in their town or village. Rodney had learned to use a tape recorder, which saved a lot of tedious note-taking and even more tedious requests for repetitions.

'Cake,' said Kit thoughtfully. 'Will there be coffee cake?'

'Now that I don't know. But there's sure to be something nice.'

There always was, when Kit appeared. He had his mother's deceptive air of fragility (though he was in fact a robust child), her feathery curls, and large, appealing hazel eyes, and nice polite manners of a slightly old-fashioned kind, instilled into him by Vi, who believed in boys learning at an early age to be little gentlemen. No doubt the village school would change all that.

Kit had survived admirably the death of Helena. His experienced father had gently prepared him for it, throwing out mild hints that she might soon be taken away for a holiday with some very cheerful angels, who were quite used to nursing people back to health and had excellent facilities for it – not quite the seaside, somewhere much nicer. A hunt through Rodney's bookcases had produced a quantity of appealing pictures of cherubim and other heavenly bodies with reassuring smiles. Doran's art books had yielded more.

'Don't let's draw his attention to the ones in the church windows – they're all Victorian, depressing and sexless.'

'Which nobody could say about the cherubs.'

'No, indeed. Why are angels nearly always sort of neuter? Blake's aren't, of course, and the ones in the Wilton Diptych are extremely feminine and really court ladies, I suppose. But mostly they wear those shift things and halfway hair.'

'I haven't the least idea, but I'll think about it. Will they work, that's the point? With Kit.'

The painted messengers had worked. So had a series of outings for Kit, valiantly and thoroughly conducted by Annabella Firle, when his half-sister was in her last illness. He had cried a good deal when told that Helena had gone when he and Annabella were out one day, and initially had suffered from withdrawal symptoms: she had done her best to spoil him. Then, a realist like all children, Kit had begun to accept Helena's absence, and gradually was forgetting.

As a baby Kit had been nursemaided by a local girl, Carole Flesher, but an attack she had incurred at Bell House, in the course of an attempted theft, had turned her off the Chelmarshes altogether. When they met in the village Carole looked the other way. She now worked at a supermarket till, a great deal safer in her opinion than being skivvy to a family where nasty things happened in connection with antique objects.

That was why Rodney took his son with him to as many Dela destinations as possible – it gave Doran some free time. And Kit was excellent company, being used to the conversation of grown-ups who had never inflicted baby-talk on him. His father had even got him into the habit of reciting works he was certainly too young to understand.

'*Sir Christopher Wren . . .*' Rodney began.

'*Went to dine wiv some men*,' Kit gravely continued.

'*He said "If anyone calls –* " '

' "*Say I'm signing Saint Paul's*" '.

'Splendid. Now, what about Rupert of the Rhine?'

'*Fought Cromwell was a swine*,' remembered Kit obediently.

'*But he felt quite sure –* '

'*After – after . . .*'

'Go on, you can remember it.'

'*After Martin Moor!*' Kit finished triumphantly.

'Great. Only it's Marston, not Martin. And don't you forget that one, because your mother and I agree with it wholeheartedly. Ah, this looks like the place.'

The shabby little Victorian house was indeed the home of Mr Beamish, the reputed authority on Sheppey's antiquities. Unfortunately his reputation for deafness and irascibility had not been exaggerated. He affected not to know who Rodney was, expressed deep distrust of the tape recorder, and seemed unwilling to part with any information – if, indeed, he had much, which Rodney began to doubt after ten minutes' struggling.

'What about Sir Robert de Shurland?' Rodney asked desperately. 'You know, Minster Abbey. The legend of Grey Dolphin.'

'We don't have dolphins round these coasts. Ought to know that.'

'Well, I do. But this was Sir Robert's horse . . .'

'Coffee cake,' said Kit, who had been sitting in thoughtful silence, ignored by Beamish.

'All nonsense,' snorted the old man. 'Just a heraldic convention, could have been a dog or a . . .'

'Coffee cake.' Kit's mouth was turning down. 'Hungry, Daddy.'

'Yes, yes, Kit, all right. We'll be going in a minute.'

Mr Beamish's strong spectacles were now focused on Kit, not benevolently.

'What's that child doing here? Who let it in? What's

it grizzling for? Get it off my clean chair, I know what these brats are like and I won't have my furniture spoiling.'

Kit's polite manners slipped, and he made a gargoylesque face. Rodney shut up his recorder, got to his feet and took Kit's hand, none too gently.

'Yes, well. Thank you, Mr Beamish, we won't trouble you any more. I'm sure you're tired.'

Recriminations were pointless. Kit knew his father well enough to sense displeasure. Rodney drove on to the next village, where a shop provided filled rolls and mass-produced individual apple pies. Informing Kit that they would be eaten later, he carried on across the Island, to its north-western tip, Warden Point. There he stopped and they picnicked on the cliffs, surrounded by hopeful screaming gulls.

The sea was a shimmering expanse, the dark green of marble, great planes of stormy grey and streaks of silver, as though shoals of fish were emigrating into the North Sea. Not a gleam of blue, for there was none in the skies. Just another English summer.

'You can get out and run about,' he told Kit, 'so long as you don't go near the road or the edge of the cliff. I'll be watching, mind.'

Kit ran off joyfully, scattering crust from his roll to lure the hovering gulls. Rodney sat on in the car, under the colourless sky, thinking colourless thoughts.

The interview with Beamish had gone wrong. It seemed he was unable to deal with a difficult old man on behalf of a second-rate radio station – he who had so many years' experience of difficult people and complex organizations, not the least of them his own Church.

But his Church had rejected him – had let him go, then taken him back on sufferance, in charge of a very small parish which one day it would decide to abandon. He saw an enormous fabric repair bill looming, for St Leonard's crumbling tower and the broken guttering which was sending down rainwater to erode the north wall. The authorities would do nothing about that, and he could do nothing about it himself.

He couldn't afford a nanny for Kit, to set Doran free full time for her own profession, which he knew she missed. But for her partner Howell Evans's businesslike running of the shop, there would be very little income from it. That could be doubled if Doran were freed.

He had been glad to see Helena's battery-operated wheelchair go when she had no more use for it. *Glad.* A daughter lost and a bit of money gained. Sitting in the car with both doors open in case Kit should need rescuing from anything, he felt all of his forty-three years, and more. He thought of his father, who had expected so much from his clever only son. He thought of Doran, who also must have expected a different kind of marriage, and here she was, married to a failure, a girl who might have attracted someone brilliant in her own line, someone who could have given her a setting worthy of her, comfort, money . . .

But Doran wasn't a girl any more.

Kit ran up to him, holding something carefully in both hands.

'Daddy, look. A snail!'

The snail was a dead crab in an extremely poor state of preservation. Rodney examined it from as far away as possible. 'You know, darling, I don't believe it's very well. I think it needs rest. Put it down over there and arrange some stones over it. Then come back and I'll wipe your hands with a tissue.'

'Poor snail.' Kit carried it tenderly away. As he buried it, he crooned a small tuneless song, one of his own making which he often sang. Doran thought he was going to be musical. Well, that would be something for Dad's old age. My son, the well-known . . . tenor? cellist? conductor? pop singer? No, that would hardly involve music.

Depressed by this thought, Rodney gazed at the cliff edge and tried to cheer himself with the thought that the cliffs were packed with fossils. Then he dredged up from his store of useless knowledge the fact that somebody had once built a church at Warden Point, out of the stones of old London Bridge, of all things.

It was not there now. Later Victorians had demolished it to stop it sliding over the crumbling cliff, but the graves of its little churchyard slowly and gruesomely descended to the beach. Even later, tourists picked up bones and took them home as souvenirs. Rodney shuddered.

It began to rain. Yes, this was the English summer all right.

'Come on, Kit,' he called. 'Time to go home.'

In the car Kit was quiet, as though his father's melancholy had passed itself on to him. After a few minutes he said reflectively, 'Nasty man didn't have coffee cake. Bad.'

'He wasn't nasty, darling. Only old and tired. Never mind, I shan't get like that just yet. I hope.'

Kit pondered, then laughed. 'Funny Daddy.'

'That's right, son. The jester with a breaking heart, that's your papa. Good Heavens, what rubbish. Take no notice. Here, have another go at this.' He handed over the mini-football game. 'You just might score.'

Doran found Howell in the room behind the shop, working out tax figures. He looked up.

'Well, well. Your *baban* let you off the string, has he?'

'Kit isn't exactly a baby, he's four, and Rodney's taken him to Sheppey. Howell, tell me something nice. Tell me some vague old person walked in with a shopping trolley full of goodies wrapped up in newspaper. A delicious little fairytale illustration from the twenties. A very small early Ralph Wood figurine, with only the tiniest repair. A nice fan, I don't care what period, I'd just like to handle one.'

'Then sell it quick? That what all this is about?' Howell waved her to a vacant chair, a pretty George II walnut in need of repair, and put away his papers methodically. He was pleased to see his partner, even if it interrupted what he was doing. Over the years he and Doran had developed a comfortable, balanced relationship, each affecting the other. He had watched her turn from a wistful, insecure girl to a mature woman, married to the man who had been her love, even then. Still trusting, open as a flower, as honest as he knew himself to be capable of becoming a human corkscrew if occasion demanded.

She had watched him mature from a somewhat shifty, lazy, corrupt person into a man aware of the dangers of the world and the worse dangers of his own nature. He had given up, since she and Rodney had been married, heavy smoking, soft drugs, and, so far as she knew, the pretty boys who had fed on his strengths and weaknesses. His reformation was not entirely due, though it would have been nice to think so, to the beautiful and ennobling influence of Doran and Rodney, but to the self-protective instincts which had belatedly wakened in the wary Welshman. Doran was glad of it. In spite of his pose as a misfit, she had found out, in peril herself, his well-concealed courage, the *gwroldeb* which had led his ancestors into innumerable battles against the invader. He was loyal and tough, where she and hers were concerned.

And he had immaculate taste and knowledge of furniture and clocks and a keen brain for a bargain. In a strange way she loved him, and he her, though neither would have acknowledged or admitted it. In another life they could have been father and daughter. He still looked like a shabby dark tabby tomcat, and his habits were untidy, but that was Howell.

'What is it, then?' he asked. 'Fed up? Want out of something? Rodney trouble?'

'No. Certainly not. I don't think he's too happy at the moment, but it isn't me. I mean, it's not him. I don't know what I mean. Except that I wish I could do a bit more trading, buying, seeing somebody who wasn't Abbotsbourne. Silly, really.'

'Yeah. I'll brew up.'

Howell's brew of tea was dark and bitter, but had its own reviving quality.

'I think it was better when Rodney was at St Crispin's, even though he loathed having to toe the line for the Barminster pundits who are practically KGB about all the things Rodney likes, like the Old Service. Well, they've got the Duttons now, and they can have the pews ripped out and coffee served between hymns and improvised addresses by unqualified ladies, if they want them.'

'You're still the parson's wife up at Elvesham, you know. Not good enough for you?' Howell put his feet, in their tattered trainers, up on the table and prepared to listen.

'Of course it is. I like Ruth Firle so much. I wish *she* lived next door, now.'

'Why, who does? Haven't been down your place recent. Last time I was, it was that tart, lots of glitz, tried to make that young cop you'd got shacked up in the nursery.'

'How depraved you make it sound – he was only on guard – after the . . .' Doran hurried on, not wanting to linger on memories of the awful time when Kit had been kidnapped and held for ransom.

'No, that was Richenda Berg – she was all right, just a bit acquisitive. This is Mrs Paula French.'

'Mrs? Ms? No mate around?'

'Oh yes, in computers or solar heating or something boring. A meek sort of man called Euan – extraordinary name – who says "Yes, Darling" all the time, and obviously worships the wall-to-wall Axminster she walks on, not to mention the very expensive vinyl on the kitchen floor. One of those TV kitchens, you know, pseudo-Tudor units, and a bottle of wine and a bowl of fruit all you ever see in the way of sordid cooking.'

Howell's moustache twitched. There was more than a touch of bitterness here. It would amuse him to find out why. And that stuff about acquisitiveness was good, coming from her, the girl who even at her most happily married couldn't keep her big soulful eyes off the sort of guy she fancied.

'Rodney like her?' he inquired casually.

'Rodney can't stand her. He says she drains his psychic energy. She poses at him and says all the cliché things people say to vicars, and she's even dragged poor old Euan out to Matins at Elvesham. Once.'

'So who's she after?'

Doran shrugged. 'Nobody that I know of. At least Richenda was honest about it. I think this one just likes to collect scalps, or imagine she's collecting them. I can just see it. Paula with a string of bleeding scalps round her belt, suddenly noticing they're spoiling her nice High Street fashion skirt. "Ooh, Euan, take these nasty things off and put them in the kitchen bin, there's a good boy." '

Howell's hoot of laughter brought her down from her flights of mimicry.

'I didn't come here to talk about blasted Paula, though. How's trade? That's a nice clock. French, ormolu, Louis Sixteen?'

'More like French, ormolu, Queen Vic just about to hop the twig. I'd put it at 1899–1900. Bit poncy, but not too bad. I'll get a good turn on that one.'

'Did you sell that mahogany drop-leaf?'

'Yeah. Got a small bomb for it. I told him what it was, said it wasn't Regency, showed him the leg that'd been off,' said Howell virtuously, 'but he didn't seem to care. Took it anyway.'

'Good.' Doran wondered what the exact truth of this story was, but knew better than to ask further. Instead, looking at her watch (though there must have been eighteen clocks in the room, quite a few of them going) she said, 'Do you think the Port Arms will be open yet?'

The pub down by the old harbour of Eastgate was low-ceilinged, smoky, held up by some genuine beams and a lot of fake ones, its inglenooks illuminated by red bulbs and adorned with an immense number of repro horse brasses, miniature brass sailing ships, fishing trophies, a collection of travellers' souvenirs (some of a distinctly vulgar nature) and theatrical photographs signed by players who had worked at the nearby Theatre Royal. The antique dealers of Eastgate congregated at the Port Arms almost to a man, or woman, or anything between the two.

'Bound to be,' Howell replied. 'Got new, civilized licensing laws, 'aven't we?'

'Then let's go and have one. Or two. Today I'm free, free!'

Doran's spirits were still reasonably high, in spite of the return of a depressed Rodney, when they set off for the evening's Parish Council meeting at Elvesham. Kit, talking of snails and gulls and an old man who was cross, was left in the charge of Vi.

The meeting was an informal fortnightly one, held at the home of Simon and Ruth Firle, a dignified neo-Georgian house in its own considerable grounds not far from the beautiful, crumbling church. Simon, who commuted to the City, was a serious, kindly man, with a high balding brow and a vague resemblance to the portraits of Shakespeare, Ruth a handsome bustling woman of eminent good sense and ability, like their daughter Annabella, who had been Helena's best friend, now doing notably well at Barminster School of Art.

The meeting was small and select. Apart from the Firles and the Chelmarshes, there were four of the elderly people who are invariably the prop of such village churches and have little else in their lives, Margaret Culffe, a dealer from Barminster and her younger brother Guy, together with a small following of Rodney's own from Abbotsbourne.

The most unlikely of these was the pork butcher, Jack Turner. An ungracious, tactiturn man, he had never been a favourite of Doran's, even if she had been able to tolerate the atmosphere of his shop, which was clean but strongly meaty. He had, however, his reasons for defecting.

'Always very strong on the Church, my parents were,' he told Rodney. 'Yes, I know I didn't turn up at St Crispin's only at Christmas, and that was because they had this blessed Rite A and Rite B and I don't know what.'

Rodney began to point out that he had been granted by his masters one service a month according to the Book of Common Prayer, but the butcher pressed on.

'So when they said you were sticking to the old ways up at Elvesham, I said to the wife, I said, "We'll go up there and show 'em." My old dad would have wanted that.'

Rodney asked no further. The human heart is a mysterious thing; it was not for him to ask why the feelings of Jack's departed old dad had not influenced him before, as the traditional service had been available at Elvesham for years. He took the Turner collection money and was thankful.

Ruth provided the company with wine instead of the usual coffee, though that was available to anyone who insisted on it. She felt that wine promoted ideas and loosened tongues, as it usually did.

'The main problem is,' said Rodney, 'the tower. The erosion is so bad that if it isn't attended to by winter it'll fall down. Just like that. We shall be stepping over a heap of rubble to get into church, those of us who didn't happen to be passing when it fell.'

'They ought to help at Barminster.' This was Mr Shoesmith, who had been churchwarden since he was a young man and was now a fairly old one. He also mowed and tended the little churchyard, and would do so until he joined its occupants.

'They don't want to know,' Ruth said. 'Simon and I have appealed to them personally, on top of all Rodney's appeals.'

'Entreaties,' said Doran. 'He practically wrote odes to them.'

'*O ponder well, be not severe*,' Rodney added.

'That's from *The Beggar's Opera*!' exclaimed old Miss Troit delightedly. 'I sang in it when I was quite a young girl. I was one of Macheath's young ladies, Sukey something. We were always getting up musical pieces in those days.'

'Then I wish you'd go and sing to them now, Miss Troit,' said Rodney. 'Who knows, your sweet voice might move their hearts. They do not, repeat not, wish to know about Elvesham. They say it's not in Pevsner, the interior was shockingly restored by a disciple of Gilbert Scott's, and the congregation is minimal.'

'That's the whole trouble,' Doran put in. 'Because there aren't enough of us, we can't raise enough money. Abbotsbourne's not going to help, is it? The farming community around aren't exactly churchgoers. None of us is rich enough to do a Carnegie out of our own pocket – are we? Surprise me, somebody.'

Everybody carefully avoided looking at Simon, the only one of them they knew to be anywhere near rich.

Ruth, who was sitting next to him, noted his worried expression and patted his hand.

'I know what you're all thinking, so don't pretend. But whatever it may look like we have a daughter to educate – expensively – and living in a hamlet like this we have to run two cars, and Simon's been pretty generous already – well, *I* think so, though we don't begrudge any of it.'

'Of course you've been generous – lavish!' Doran said. 'We can't expect you to carry the whole thing. And everybody else has been wonderful, helping with coffee mornings and things.' She had sacrificed a very nice Victorian canterbury, an appropriate object in the circumstances, for the sake of the church, to which she gave the price it had fetched. 'But what more can we do?'

Nobody said anything.

'More wine?' Simon began to circulate with bottles of red and white.

Miss Troit drank her second glass like somebody thoroughly used to it. Ruth watched Maggie Culffe knock back her fourth like someone even more thoroughly used to it, which she was. Maggie could get out of hand – Ruth touched her husband's arm and gave a little shake of the head in Margaret's direction.

But it was Miss Troit who, Bacchus-fired, spoke up.

'You know I mentioned those musical pieces we used to get up in the village hall, when I was a girl? Well, they were for charity, and they went down awfully well and everybody seemed to want to be in them. Why don't we do one for our church?'

She beamed round the company expectantly.

Doran said, 'But Miss Troit, who . . .'

Ruth sat up straight. 'That's a brilliant idea, Miss Troit. Why don't we do one, indeed? Why don't we do a Gilbert and Sullivan?'

2

I have a song to sing, O

Everybody was too polite to say 'You're mad!' but the words might as well have been spoken, so eloquent were the faces. Margaret laughed, Simon looked acutely embarrassed at being let down in public by his dependable Ruth, Rodney seemed not to believe his ears, Will Shoesmith silently mouthed the names over and over, as though trying out some unfamiliar form of prayer.

It was left to Doran to speak for them.

'Ruth – don't you think we'd be – well, over-ambitious? I mean, there aren't enough of us, even if we roped in outsiders. And some of us can't sing. *I* can't, for one.'

'I'm not suggesting that we put on a performance of the entire *Ring* cycle. I happen to agree with Miss Troit – musicals are still popular – look at the sell-out shows in London and on Broadway – and in G. and S. you don't even need a lot of trained singers, amateurs do them all the time.'

'Well, yes, but . . .'

'As for using outsiders, of course we'd have to. We've all got friends, haven't we? Annabella certainly has hordes of them. Then there are people in Abbotsbourne – you could scrape some up, I'm sure, Jack.'

The butcher looked gloomy. His Christmas card list was not extensive.

'If we poached any Abbotsbourne churchgoers,' Rodney said, 'Edwin Dutton would personally kill me, or have me excommunicated, or something.'

'He can't,' Doran said. 'It's not in the rules. All he could do would be to put on a rival show, and I can't see him doing that, can you?'

It was indeed hard to visualize the grave vicar of St Crispin's in the role of Kappelmeister. Possibly of *Joseph and his Amazing Technicolor Dreamcoat*, Doran reflected. But it wouldn't be exactly jolly.

'What about the musicians? – we'd need an orchestra.'

'My old school, Duke Humphrey's,' murmured Guy Culffe, with his shy hint of a stammer, 'they've got a smashing orchestra. I know the man who . . . you could talk to him, Maggie, couldn't you?'

'He's a terrible bore, but anything for you, darling.' She dabbed a vinous kiss on her brother's cheek.

Rodney was beginning to take fire. 'Radio Dela – now that's an idea. Jim Fontenoy must have plenty of contacts – I could ask him. He's such a roaring enthusiast he'd probably want to join in himself.'

Some objections were raised. It was early July, coming up to the holiday period, when people would be going away and wouldn't be interested in amateur stage shows. The boys of Guy's old school would be breaking up soon for the summer recess. Besides, where would they get the costumes? None of them had production experience – who would pull the show together? Everybody was talking at once. Rodney's voice topped them all.

'Stop arguing and listen.'

They turned to him.

'It's quite clear to me,' he said, 'that in spite of all these ifs and buts there's a general excitement and enthusiasm in this room for putting on a Gilbert and Sullivan production. It wouldn't cost much, if we're clever – and it would do something, if not all, for poor old St Leonard's. To my mind, it's as good as on stage already. And it would be a lot of fun.'

Doran clapped her hands, as much because Rodney's dark cloud seemed to have lifted as from her own enthusiasm. It *would* be fun. Already she was mentally organizing babysitters for Kit and canvassing possible singers among her Eastgate colleagues.

'So all I ask you,' Rodney continued, 'is *which* Gilbert and Sullivan?'

Doran kept quiet, knowing Rodney's thought processes. But she had opened her lips to say 'There's one that – ' when he said it for her.

'It seems obvious to me. Small cast, dramatic story, nobody has to be desperately funny, no patter songs, straightforward music – all right, what is it?'

'*The Yeomen of the Guard*,' said Ruth. 'Of course! Why didn't I think of it?'

'Because it was so obvious, like the clues in all the best whodunits,' Rodney replied.

The somewhat dazed committee having gone home, Rodney and Doran stayed on at the Firles' for what they thought of as a proper drink.

'I can't believe it,' Doran said. 'Such a ridiculous, ambitious project. And yet it seems the right one, in its peculiar way.'

'It does, it does.' Rodney recalled, with something like a superstitious thrill, how he had that day idly spoken of himself to Kit as a jester with a breaking heart. Jack Point, of course. But why should Point have been in his mind at that moment? *It is sung to the moon by a love-lorn loon, who fled from the mocking throng, O* . . . Absolutely irrelevant.

'I should like,' he said modestly, 'to be Point.'

'Of course,' said Ruth.

'Of course,' echoed Simon. Doran studied her husband anew, as she often did, and saw that he was indeed Point. Cheerful, amiable, he could teach his congregation with a quip, or trick them into learning with a laugh, just as Point boasted. He could also be deeply melancholy, the doleful merryman moping mum. It would do him a world of good to act it out.

'What about the other parts?' she asked. 'There aren't many principals, but they're important. Let's see: time, Henry VIII's England, place, the Tower of London. Sergeant Meryll, who runs the Yeomen of the Guard, has a prisoner, Colonel Fairfax, charged with – witchcraft, I think – and due for the chop.'

'Literally,' added Rodney.

'He's got a daughter, Phoebe, who's a bit randy and engaged to horrible Wilfred Shadbolt, the head jailer.'

'And Assistant Tormentor,' Rodney said.

'You seem to know it all,' Simon remarked, admiring.

'All from the printed page, no experience, absolutely no Equity card. Reading maketh a full man, as Bacon said.'

'We might have known,' Ruth said briskly. 'Well, then a couple of strolling players arrive, Jack Point and Elsie Maynard, who are sort-of-engaged, but – what happens then, Doran?'

'Elsie's hauled off to marry the prisoner Fairfax so that his fortune won't go to the nasty cousin – '

'Sir Clarence Poltwhistle,' Rodney couldn't resist adding.

'All right, Gilbert was sticking his neck out with that one. Anyway, it all gets very complicated after that, with the Sergeant's son changing places with Fairfax. Then . . .'

Ruth had been waiting for her moment.

'If I might suggest something – I'd really like to play Dame Carruthers.'

'Housekeeper to the Tower. But you aren't old enough,' Doran said.

'Thank you, dear. She's a fearful old hag and a battleaxe, and I know there are people who'd say the part would fit me like a glove – don't leap to my defence, Simon, I know I can be bossy at times – but she does have a noble opening song about the Tower. I – though I say it, I haven't a bad voice.'

'She has a beautiful contralto,' Simon told them proudly. 'We met in a church choir, when women were first allowed to sing in them.'

'Good.' Rodney knew about Simon's own robust baritone, which was the pride of St Leonard's very small and erratic choir. He turned to Doran. 'What about you? Elsie? Phoebe? Both nice girls – in their way.'

'I did tell everybody – I can't sing. Not a note that would reach to the back of the Old Primary School – I suppose we *are* thinking of the Old Primary School?' she asked Rodney.

'Where else? It's got a stage, two side entrances, wings, and two separate dressing rooms with the usual conveniences. It's proved perfectly adequate for school nativity plays, not that they demand a lot of scenery or props, though someone did paint a splendid Star one year on a huge piece of canvas.'

'Annabella!' cried Doran excitedly. 'She can paint a great Tower, and we can use it as a permanent backcloth. Don't you agree, Ruth?'

'Certainly. She could do that on her ear – and if she got some friends to help her, we could have a fabulous set. I'll ask her as soon as she comes in.'

'I'm still a bit exercised about Elsie and Phoebe, if Doran won't play,' Rodney reflected. 'I can't think offhand of any girls round here.'

'But we don't necessarily want girls from round here,' Doran pointed out. 'If we hog all the principal roles ourselves, outsiders won't want to be hauled in just for chorus parts. We must have a bit of bait to dangle – Fairfax, Shadbolt, Phoebe and Elsie, Leonard

Meryll – we've got to offer them around, when we're doing chorus auditions.'

'Which will be extremely dicey and difficult to arrange, but I think I can do it, if I twist Chapman's arm.' Ralph Chapman was the organist at St Crispin's and by no means a favourite of Edwin Dutton's, having a strong resistance to the modern hymn tunes and hooray-for-God songs which his vicar constantly demanded of him. Bell House had a good piano, Chapman was a friend . . . it might be organized.

Ruth suddenly yawned. 'Oh dear! I'm sorry, I didn't mean to be rude. Don't all go.'

But everyone, it seemed, had had enough. Warm, excited, stimulated by Simon's good whisky, Doran and Rodney returned to their car.

'I'll drive,' Doran told him. 'I've had less than you, and we don't want to lose our Point to drink-drive bans, do we.' She fastened her seat belt, giggling. 'I've just had a marvellous casting idea.'

'What?'

'The Headsman who comes on at the end of Act One to execute Fairfax.'

'Well, who?'

'Jack Turner, of course! Who else would be as handy with an axe?'

As though some celestial backer were behind the production, the plans so impulsively made went forward with sleek precision. The manager of Radio Dela just happened to know a 'resting' theatre director, Max Johnston, who was not too pressed for income and agreed to direct the show on an expenses-only basis. He was a Scotsman of a slightly uncertain temper, and he had the advantage of having directed Gilbert and Sullivan before, for a mushroom company which had toured the United States and Australia for a season.

He was devoted to his wife, Amy, a sweet and pretty

woman with the voice of an angel, who was almost perpetually in work with one or the other of the opera companies. Max fretted because she was fully engaged at present singing in Viennese Nights here and there in and around London.

'She'd have made a great Phoebe,' he lamented. 'I'd love to have worked on that with her. The emotion she can get into that part! *When a brother leaves his sister For another, sister weeps* . . . Man! It could have been Butterfly, Marguerite, Violetta.'

'I'm sure,' Rodney agreed. 'But you see, we just can't afford professional singers. It's purely your kindness in only taking expenses that allows us to have you, Max.'

'Aye, well. I'll be doing the Festival piece at the cathedral next month. Might as well get to know the district.'

The telephone rang. Doran answered it.

A light, teasing male voice at the other end uttered Doran's unfavourite start to a telephone conversation.

'Guess who?'

'I can't guess who,' she answered sharply. 'Just tell me.'

'You mean you don't recognize the teones of an aeuld reomance?'

Doran took a deep breath. 'If you'd stop talking in that silly way, we might get somewhere. Now come on, who are you?'

'Not just another dirty caller. It's Rupert.'

'Rupert Wylie? What do you want? We aren't looking for a new house, in case you've got one for sale.'

'Oh, I have, pet, hundreds, new private estates mushrooming, as we say. Can't I persuade you to leave that poor old Queen Anne wreck, which we will sell for you at an astronomical profit, and buy something nice and upmarket?'

'No, you can't, and I'm busy.'

'Yes, I know. You're an impresario now. Into musicals.'

'Oh. You don't mean you're interested, yourself?'

'I am, passionately. I want a part. Love dressing up in cossie. And I *can* sing. Didn't know that, did you?'

'No. What experience have you had?'

'I was in a band for three years. Did the vocals. We never got into the charts so we buried it. And I was Woof in a university production of *Hair* – terribly old-fashioned, of course, but these quaint old pieces seem to pull 'em in. Listen.' He rendered, in a clear, rather twangy tenor, the opening lines of 'Good Morning Starshine'. It was not, on the whole, bad.

'Mm. Are you serious about this, Rupert, or is it just that you're bored at the moment?'

'How can you wrong me like that? Of course I'm interested, or I wouldn't be wasting the firm's valuable time calling you.'

'Okay. You'll have to audition. No, it isn't that we've got a surplus of talent, you'll have to audition, that's all.' She gave him time and place, adding, 'Does this go for Fenella, too?'

'God, no. She'd be a total loss. Anyway, she's in pod again.'

'In what?'

'In farrow, in pup, whatever you like to call it.'

In foal, Doran silently thought, would be most apt, Rupert's aristocratic wife's resemblance to an extremely expensive racehorse being even more pronounced than it had been. She murmured congratulations and rang off.

Useful to gain another man for the cast, but she would rather it had not been Rupert. However ridiculous it might seem in today's climate, she still felt uncomfortable at the memory of her brief seduction by Rupert, years ago, before her marriage. If she had been sober, instead of completely stoned and silly after dining with him at a faked-up country restaurant. If the actual seduction had been somewhere other than the back of Rupert's BMW. If she had not been so much in love with Rodney – hopelessly, it had seemed then – that the whole episode was a betrayal of him as well as of herself.

The Oast, where they had dined that night, was gone now, turned into a private house. Doran was glad.

Rodney, who had wandered out of the room during the telephone conversation, returned.

'Rupert, was that?'

'It was. Offering himself as a tenor. He's not too bad, allowing for telephone distortion – it takes the bass out of voices, doesn't it? Anyway, I think he might make a Fairfax, if nobody better turns up.'

'Oh, good.' Rodney knew about the Rupert incident, though not the details: no priest could have failed to know, with such a transparently honest woman as Doran. He had never given the slightest sign that he knew.

Max's comment on the news that they had a possible Colonel Fairfax was terse.

'Aye, well. The man's a stick, one of Gilbert's stuffed dummies. It'll not matter too much who sings him, with only two solos. We could even cut "Free from his fetters grim", it's dropped sometimes. In the circumstances it'll be a mercy if we get a passable performance out of any of the bunch I've seen so far.'

When he had left, Rodney shook his head, fingering notes on the piano which was now perpetually open for auditionees.

'In the caircumstances it'll be a maircy if the thing gets done at all,' he said, exaggerating Max's Lowland accent.

'Oh, nonsense. I've been agreeably surprised at what we've got up to now. Anyway, you were there at the meeting, you agreed. In fact, it was your idea. I thought you were all enthusiasm. I must admit,' Doran added a trifle sharply, sensing another of Rodney's melancholic moods coming on, 'I was astonished that you were in favour – or knew all that much about G. and S. We've never talked about the works. I thought your operatic taste stopped at *Hugh the Drover*.'

'Oh, it does, it's the only one I've appeared in, when I was about fifteen. *Like true-born Cotswold men, brave boys, like true-born Cotswold men*,' he hummed, with, Doran suspected, deliberate tunelessness. 'I know the words of *Yeomen* better than the music. Really rather well.'

'Of course. Not exactly opera, though, is it?'

'Depends on one's standards.'

'I thought mine were rather high.' We're almost fighting, Doran thought.

They avoided catching each other's eye.

'I'm going to the shops,' Doran said. 'Kit's at Jonathan's till half past twelve. Fetch him if I'm not back. Anything you want?'

'No, thanks.'

Abbotsbourne's little square of shops was all colour and warmth, half an hour to noon. Its windows glowed with summer vegetables and flowers, local produce from market gardens and private ones. A new, tiny, ambitious boutique advertised world-famous fashion names with glittering jewellery and two dresses. Doran studied them, with a reckless desire to buy something, anything. But they were both outrageously expensive and hideous, outdated in design, more suitable for an archdeacon's mother than for a person only just turned thirty.

She turned her back on them and ran straight into the arms of her next-door neighbour.

The lady of Magnolia House looked exactly as the writers of the top Sunday fashion supplements would have wished her to look. An inch or so taller than

Doran, just above middle height for a woman, she gave the impression of endless legs and a flawless figure, just as her dress, of silky cotton the colour of young apples, conveyed casual elegance. It was a difficult colour to wear, but she made it look easy.

Doran hoped her smile of greeting matched the dazzler she was receiving from Paula. The sun brought bronze glints from a silky head of short smooth hair, dashingly cut in a fringe like the hair of the beautiful Louise Brooks in one of the thirties films Rodney had on video.

'Doran, what a *wonderful* morning!' The warmth of tone implied that Doran was personally responsible for it.

'Yes, marvellous.' There must be something original to add, but Doran's mind went blank, as it tended to do in Paula's company. She managed a compliment on the apple-green frock. Paula modestly lowered her long lashes – surely not all natural? Her sunglasses were of the kind which tint to a delicate deep rose, yet leave the eye glamorously visible.

'Oh, this. Actually, I ran it up myself. I find it so much simpler to choose one's own style and exactly the right material. Don't you think?'

'Of course. I'd do it myself, but I can't sew at all. If I turn a hem up it comes unstitched straight away. I don't even have time.'

Paula's pretty laugh rang like the chime of one of the French clocks Howell despised. 'I shouldn't have time, should I, what with thinking up something nice and new for Euan's dinner every evening, and embroidering my chair-seats (did I show you, Queen Mary's own pattern?) and redecorating? Oh yes, I've decided to re-do the whole house in the most gorgeous paper you ever saw, flowers, flowers, flowers . . .'

She sketched them in the air with a gesture which showed off immaculate nail varnish. Doran looked round for an escape route, but Paula all but stepped in front of her.

'You're coming to the lecture this evening, of course? I know – we'll go together in my car, that will save you all the driving. If I honk outside your gate at seven o'clock that should give us plenty of time – '

'What lecture? Where?' Doran asked desperately.

Paula wrinkled her brow in the slightest of frowns, guaranteed not to cause lines.

'But you must know about it – it's just your subject. The English Miniaturists and their Art, at the Poly in Eastgate. You've just forgotten.'

'I haven't. I don't see the Polytechnic's syllabuses, syllabi, whatever. I simply haven't time, Paula.'

'Oh dear. What a pity. You should, you know, it would broaden your knowledge, and you can't have too much of that in your trade. I'm doing the whole Advanced Art course, did I tell you?'

'No. Goodness, is that the time?' Doran glanced at her watch a fraction after the exclamation, but she was sure Paula failed to notice, or appeared not to notice. She was smiling kindly.

'Well, see you tomorrow evening, anyway. Don't tell me you've forgotten *that*.'

Doran, backing away, paused. As with Juliet, she felt a faint cold fear thrill through her veins.

'Forgotten what?'

'The auditions,' Paula explained patiently. 'At your house. Max was enchanted when I offered myself.'

If Doran went on parroting Paula's final words they were going to sound like an old music-hall crosstalk act. The awful truth was dawning on her.

'I hardly knew him before, but when I heard he was staying here for the production I remembered we'd met, one of Radio Dela's parties, I think, something like that, so I dropped in at the Rose and he very sweetly asked me for a drink, and I sang to him. Just like that. Everybody in the bar stopped talking and listened, very flattering.'

'What did you sing?' Doran heard her words coming out as a croak.

'Oh – something from *The Pirates*. "Poor Wandering One". You may not know it.'

Of course I know it, you fool, and it happens to be one of my particular dislikes, and if you start trilling it here I shan't be responsible for my actions. Aloud, Doran answered restrainedly, 'Yes, I do. Was Max impressed?'

'Well, he doesn't *say* very much, but I could see that he was. Anyway, he told me to come along tomorrow evening and try out one of the numbers from this production. Just a formality.'

Impossible to say 'I shan't let you in'. Doran smiled, with some difficulty, and escaped.

To Rodney, who was giving Kit his lunch in the garden, she exploded.

'You're not going to believe this.' Out came the dreadful tale. Kit listened, wide-eyed. Rodney looked more and more dispirited.

'The mere thought of having that woman in the cast turns me quite ill,' she raged. 'She's a monster. Trying to teach me my own job – "can't have too much knowledge in your trade", indeed! I know more about English miniaturists than she would if you put her in irons and lectured her with illustrations for eighteen months. And as for walking in on Max at the Rose – I bet she'd never met him before, she'd just seen him in the distance at a party or the theatre or something. Lies, all lies!'

'I should keep your voice down,' Rodney suggested. 'She does live next door, you know.'

'Mrs French,' said Kit brightly. 'She's the lady next door. I go and find her for Mummy?'

'Not if you value your life,' said his father. 'If you've

quite finished your pudding you can go and play in the tree-house. And Kit – Mummy didn't mean Mrs French, she was just talking about something grown-up. Run along, now.' Kit went happily off to the tree in whose lower branches, almost on the ground, Rodney had built a safe platform with a free-hanging wooden roof. Kit played there in all weathers, talking to imaginary characters who shared it with him.

'Oh dear.' Doran lowered her tones. 'I didn't mean to shout. And one shouldn't criticize other people in front of children. But I really was steamed up, Rod. Can't we pull out of it? We're all amateurs except Max, and there's always a troublemaker even in professional companies. And she's one, I know. It'll be a disaster.'

Rodney was himself dismayed, but someone had to keep calm.

'Why not ring Max and ask him if any of this is true?'

Max was out. But half an hour later his dark brown voice, as Doran thought of it, confirmed her fears. On the telephone it was even more Scottish: the Wee Free prophet of doom in the pulpit.

'Aye, she did. No, I don't remember her at all. Maybe we met somewhere, sometime, I don't take note of faces if I'm not working with them.'

'But her voice, Max? Can she sing, or is it all a tale?'

'She's had lessons.'

'She's had lessons in everything!' Doran broke out hysterically. 'I mean, is she any good?'

'No' bad. As good as you'll get in an amateur bunch. A bit hooty. Too much shake. Calls herself a coloratura, but she'll not make Covent Garden.'

'Good. I hope she won't make the Old Primary School.'

'To be fair, I was a wee bit impressed with the way she barged in to interview me. I thought it suggested a potential for stage confidence.'

'A potential for bloody brass neck, if you ask me. Oh well, never mind, we'll just have to hope she makes a fool of herself tomorrow night.'

Tomorrow night. Rodney wandered out into the garden after supper. In the house there was music, Doran watching a television programme to which the background was not the usual electronic racket, but a soft nostalgic blend of string and wind instruments. Lutes, he was sure, were among them. The melancholic lute . . .

In a summer night sky hardly dark the moon hung full, tonight more gold than silver, a great distant orange obscured fitfully by drifting clouds. She was the Midsummer Moon, according to the old calendar, the moon with Sirius rising beside her, Sirius the hound of Orion the Hunter, brightest star in the heavens, Homer's 'evil star', the star who brings in the Dog Days.

A magic time. Rodney was excited, uneasy, apprehensive; he had no idea why. He went indoors, closed the French windows to keep out inquisitive, doomed moths. Doran was lying on the sofa, her face soft and dreaming, watching flickering images.

He shook his head to get the miasmas out of it, and poured himself a stiffish whisky.

3

Strange adventure

Doran hoped her drawing room floor would bear the weight. It was not a large room, and it was full. Delicate old chairs supported bodies they were not made for, all the largest people having unerringly made for the most fragile seats. However, if they all crashed through into the cellar it wouldn't be far to fall.

Max himself played for the auditions. Doran had hinted to him that he might try Ruth first, to encourage the others. Ruth obligingly gave him a robust rendering of Dame Carruthers' 'When our gallant Norman foes' in her impressive contralto. He stopped her after the first verse.

'Thank you. Okay. Ye might enjoy the screw-twisting and the rack-turning a bit more, Mrs Firle. The old dame's a bit of a sadist or she'd not have got the job.'

'Oh, yes. Of course I must.' The thought seemed to come to Ruth as a new one, benevolent as she was by nature. Max scanned the expectant faces.

'Right. What about a hero? Any Colonel Fairfaxes on parade?'

His bushy eyebrows swerved towards Guy Culffe, to Doran's dismay. Guy was young and personable, certainly. With his delicate features and longish waving hair he made his elder sister Maggie look mannish. Unlike hers, his fair complexion was unmarred by over-enthusiastic drinking. Doran thought him like the portraits of Rupert Brooke, and wondered whether he were, well, someone who would interest Howell. His eyes had been fixed unmovingly on Paula ever since her entrance. He jumped as Max addressed him.

'You. Have a shot at this.'

Guy rose to go to Max's side at the piano. His hand lingered for a fraction of time in Maggie's, whether it was he or she who held the clasp.

Max played the prelude to Fairfax's opening number. Guy made a false start, and glanced at Paula, not at Max, in apology.

Doran, Rodney and Ruth interchanged glances of doubt. He can't do it, their eyes said.

He couldn't. He trembled visibly. His sweet but piping tenor began waveringly.

'*Is life a boon?*
If so, it must befall
That Death, whene'er he call,
Must call too soon.
Though fourscore years he give,
Yet one would pray to live
Another noon . . .'

Guy faltered and lost his place in the music. Max prompted him loudly.

'*What kind of plaint have I –* '

'*Who perish in July?*' Guy continued bravely. But he had turned scarlet and lost his place completely.

Max took his hands off the keys.

'Sit down, laddie, sit down. It was a try. Thanks.' He turned round to address the company, as Guy retreated, obviously on the verge of tears.

'No blame attached to that, but it's not the way. No. Did ye know, Giles – '

'Guy,' corrected Maggie, loudly and crossly.

'Guy, sorry. Did ye know Sullivan had three separate shots at setting those words? Gilbert didn't like any of 'em, said they weren't right for what was meant to be a Tudor ballad. Well, true enough, they weren't, old Gilbert knew a lot, but the tune Sullivan kept has been a winner for a hundred years. It's about a brave man, ye see, sentenced to death and making the best of it. *What kind of plaint have I, Who perish in July? I might have had to die, Perchance, in June.* But it wouldn't have worked to do a Tudor pastiche the way Sullivan parroted opera and ballet and God knows what. So Fairfax sings a song that fits into a Victorian drawing room. Fairfax is a soldier, he's got to sound like one, and never mind the score. He's got to go against the music. Anyone feel they could do that?'

'I could,' said Rupert Wylie.

'I thought Guy was sweet,' Paula observed in an audible aside to Maggie. He sent her a wavering, near-tearful smile. Doran wondered if they already knew each other, or if Guy took sudden violent amorous fancies.

'There,' Maggie consoled her brother. 'You were good. Never mind him.'

Rupert stood up straight and tall by the piano. His shoulders were broad and his muscles visible under the thin cotton T-shirt and designer jeans, worn dangerously tight. He played most outdoor sports from rugger to squash, and glowed with health. His portrait could have smiled from a poster saying 'Join the Army and look like me'.

He also sang impressively. It was not *bel canto*, it was not great art, but it was clear, and closely based on the music-line.

Max let him sing the second verse. Then he said, 'Okay. We'll have to work on your diction.' Rupert sat down, looking pleased with himself. He threw Doran a lecherous wink, to which she returned a stony stare.

His gaze wandered on to Paula, who was not looking at him, but at her score. He transferred the gaze to Ruth. Startled, she stared back into the full blaze of Rupert's smile. Not even flattered, she looked away.

Rupert sulked for a moment, but no more.

Paula was at the piano. Firmly she flipped over the pages of the music and pointed. Max began to play.

She's cheated, thought Doran. She's got the score out of Eastgate Library and swotted it up. Well, not exactly cheating, but sharp practice. And giving it the full works . . .

''Tis done! I am a bride! Oh, little ring,
That bearest in thy circlet all the gladness . . .'

warbled Paula, giving every note more than its full value and every vowel powers it never knew it had.

The aria ranged in emotion from startled joy to bitter grief to sad reflection.

'O weary wives,
Who widowhood would win,
Rejoice, rejoi-i-ice that ye have time
To weary in.'

Never had the last *weary* had so many shakes and quivers in it. Sullivan would have been surprised. Gilbert would have snorted. Paula's audience looked dazed, as she favoured them with a smiling all-round bow.

'Yes . . .' Max too looked a little dazed. 'Ye've had coaching?'

'Quite a bit, in voice-production. From Madame – but you wouldn't have heard of her.' A put-down for Madame, or for Max?

'Aye, well, it'll be grand for keeping the chorus on their toes.'

For a second or so Paula didn't reply. She was unsmiling now.

'I thought these were auditions for principals.'

'They are, supposing we get the right principals.'

Paula bridled. Doran had never seen the action so vividly illustrated, a mettlesome mare sharply pulled up by the bridle, tossing her mane and rolling her eyes. It was unlike Paula to take notice of a snub, but this was an emphatic put-down.

She said, 'But I've just auditioned for Elsie Maynard.'

'Elsie Maynard. Well, now. I wouldn't say ye were quite an Elsie Maynard, Mrs French.'

'Why not?'

Doran noted the sudden look of shock on Euan French's face. Embarrassment for his wife? Fear of some hysterical scene when they got home? The others looked generally nervous, embarrassed, Ruth and Rupert amused. Max's mouth was assuming its steel-trap line.

'Elsie was a very young girl. She was young and strong enough to tramp the roads, sing in the open air, dance for the crowds and put up with it when they chucked dead cats and rotten eggs at her. She did tumbling acts, she was a trained acrobat. In my production she'll be very physical. I don't think you're in the least suitable.'

Paula jumped from her chair. Her face was a Medusa mask. Her husband half rose to pull her down, but she shook him off, advancing on Max, who was still at the piano.

'Are you implying I'm not young enough?'

'I am. You see,' Max explained kindly, 'if she looks young they'll believe she's fit enough to do all those things. If her voice isn't great, it doesn't matter all that much. It's the illusion – '

'What do you know about illusion? For a theatre person it strikes me that you've no imagination at all. I'm thirty-three, and with proper lighting I could look twenty-three, or thirteen, if that's what you want!' She moved from side to side, displaying her slim waist, shaking her hair.

'Paula, please darling – ' She seemed not to hear Euan, any more than a boxer in a tense fight would hear a heckler among the watching crowd.

'I'm sorry, I don't see it,' returned Max impassively.

Paula seemed to stop breathing for a moment. Collecting her forces, getting ready for a comeback.

'Phoebe Meryll?' she asked Max, at last. 'Were you thinking of me for Phoebe?'

'No, I was not. Most of the same objections apply.'

Doran was by now almost sorry for Paula.

'Paula, Max,' she said firmly, 'I'm sure you can talk this out in private. Shall we go on with the rest of the auditions, or stop for refreshments, or what? Only I don't want this argument to go on.'

'I don't care what you do. You can all go to Hell,' Paula snapped, and walked out of the room. Euan rose and followed her, looking at no one. They heard the front door shut with a crash.

'Aye, well, shall we get on?' Max said.

The calm of the rest of the evening had undercurrents. Simon bashfully asked if he might swop characters, and be the brutal Wilfred Shadbolt, instead of the upright Sergeant Meryll. Everybody laughed at the thought of the serious, respectable Simon being a professional Head Jailer and Assistant Tormentor, but Doran thought Ruth looked put out, though all she said was, 'You won't have your duet with me, after all.'

'No. But I think I'll enjoy being evil for a change. You'd understand that, Rodney?'

'Oh, I do. It was why there was such a scramble to be the Devil in miracle plays. Purgation for the passions.'

Hugo Snaresby, the Eastgate solicitor who lived in Elvesham, volunteered to take on Sergeant Meryll. He was large, stuffy, and had little sense of humour, but he had a reasonable baritone voice and would look well in costume. Ralph Chapman, the organist of St Crispin's, was the Lieutenant of the Tower. All the mature parts were now filled, but candidates for the younger ones were sadly lacking. Yvonne Brigg, a friend of Annabella's, volunteered for either Elsie or Phoebe, but her voice proved to be almost inaudible, to her bitter disappointment. She shrank into a corner, and during the refreshment interval disappeared.

At the same time Maggie told Doran, 'I'm taking Guy home. No future in sitting about, is there, if you're not going to use him.'

'Oh, don't go, Maggie, please! I'm sure Max will find something for him. You want to stay, don't you, Guy?'

'Not now,' he muttered.

'What on earth did he mean?' Doran watched their departure with some relief. Maggie in drink could be unpleasant. There had been a party thrown by a Barminster dealer at which she had shown a violent side to her nature.

'I think,' Rodney said, 'I think he was slightly bewitched by the tempestuous Paula. And she did say he was sweet.'

'Oh dear. I was afraid it was something like that.' Doran caught Max's sleeve. 'Couldn't you do anything at all for Guy, Max? It would help him so much to feel a part of something – which he isn't now.'

'Why, what's the matter with him?'

'Just inadequate, I think. He's only Maggie's half-brother, really, their father married again and then Guy's own mother died and Guy broke out and got sacked from school six years ago. Then something happened she doesn't talk about. I have a feeling drugs came into it, but I'm sure he isn't on them now. Maggie's had a tough time looking after him, but she did it, and got him a job of sorts, with some photocopying firm.'

Max was thoughtful. He was a kind man at heart, and he had produced some fairly inadequate singers in his time.

'I could give him a bit of coaching for Leonard

Meryll. Not that he's got the virility. But there's not a lot of it about in this bunch, apart from Rodney and von Rupert.'

'Max, you're lovely – thank you.'

'If you women'll make him keep his shoulders back and look folk in the eye.'

'Oh, we will, don't worry. As for Paula, good riddance. You'll have to shop around for your Elsie and Phoebe, I fear. I'll put an ad in the post office window, if you like, or the stationer's, and another down near the Port Arms in Eastgate. With a theatre just round the corner it ought to be a good catchment area for rising young juveniles.'

'Mmphm. If they look good they can't sing, and if they can sing . . .'

'I know, they look like Daughter of Dracula. Never mind, we'll sort it out. Don't give up, Rodney, Judgement Day isn't at hand.'

'Isn't it? Good. I don't know why I feel that dark danger hangs upon the deed, as the Trio goes in Act One. It's an innocent enough piece of fun, putting on an entertainment for the locals. Always good for a laugh, amateur theatricals. Trouble is, this is a tragedy. I felt this evening it might be spilling over.'

'It's only because people were cross. Now: we've got more on our minds than Rodney's forebodings. Costumes. Sets. When does Annabella start and if she's not available who's going to paint this backcloth? And what am I going to do about a babysitter for Kit, every evening for three weeks? Come on, suggestions, please?'

As neither man had any suggestions, it was left to Doran to sort out all the problems.

The answers lay in Eastgate, and fellow dealers. Howell was not helpful at first.

'What you're lookin' for is theatrical merchants. Guys who loan stuff out for a production, charge you an arm and a leg for it, and if you damage any you end up limbless.'

'Great. Where does one find them?'

'Oh – there's some round Primrose Hill, plenty round Covent Garden. Easy, really.'

'But . . . who's going to spend time in London looking for them, and hand over the deposits, and bring them to Elvesham, and pay for them?' She laughed, a hollow melodramatic laugh. 'No, don't answer that. I am.'

'Couldn't you send Rod up to scout round?'

'Oh, certainly – he'd hire a chasuble, or a thurible, or an alb, or something we'd never expect him to hire, nothing to do with the production at all, and then wander into quite a different shop and buy himself a Book of Hours with money that doesn't exist. No, not Rodney.'

'All right. Take the van. Have a shufti at Covent Garden, use the NCP multi-storey in Shaftesbury Avenue, take a chance on wherever else you park, and I'll pay any tickets you collect. Straight, I will. My bit towards the show.'

Howell returned to his book of codes for the prices of objects in their shop.

'Thanks,' Doran murmured. 'Very generous.' Out in the picturesque pedestrianized street, where shops which had once been retailers of equally pedestrian goods were now either antique shops, souvenir shops, or modest boutiques, the air and the pavement were equally hot. Doran thought of the streets of London, the fumes, the ceaseless roar and rush of traffic, the hordes of wandering tourists, the hauling of objects to her precariously parked van.

'No,' she said, and went round the corner, where her friends Meg and Peg Rye lived over their shop. The premises downstairs were virtually an old-clo' store, with a fusty ambience suggesting a charity sale.

But Doran knew that Meg had a hawk's eye for good materials and clothes that would sell. Garments of every period from Victorian upwards, and some older than that, hung close-packed from the dress-rails. Doran pulled one out. Fake Georgian, not fake Tudor, but that would have been too much to hope for.

Meg herself appeared, a tiny bundly person, dressed in a little-girl summer frock from the thirties with a ribbon bow in her untidy knotted-up hair.

'Hello,' she said. 'Pet. Gorgeous to see you. Phoo, isn't it hot and stuffy?'

'It is. That's why I'm here.' She told Meg about the production. 'So knowing that you buy up old theatre stock, costumes anyway, I wondered if you could fit up a Tudor show.'

Meg pursed her small mouth. 'Tudor. Sorry, angel. There was a *Merrie England* one going a couple of years ago but the moths got to it first.'

'You've got nothing that would look remotely Tudor, if we worked on it?'

'Not a sausage. It's awkward, you see, with all those peascod-bellied doublets and farthingales and bum-rolls, they don't sort of fit into other styles if you unpick and remake them. No, I can't think of anything.' She took a red lace blouse from a rack.

'This has got high shoulders and sort of leg-of-mutton sleeves. I suppose you could team it up with a long skirt . . . No?'

'No. And we need all those men's costumes – why did any of us think this was a good idea?'

'Well, we're all a bit mad, aren't we?' She called upstairs. 'Peg!'

Her husband appeared. Today his obligatory nautical costume was represented only by a striped T-shirt and bright blue trousers, but he had plaited his longish hair into a pigtail. Doran wondered if he went as far as tarring it.

'Advice wanted, Peg,' said his wife. She outlined the problems. The pigtail rotated sadly.

'Nothing like that. Now if it was furniture . . .'

'But it is! As well, I mean. I was going up to town to hunt for both that and the costumes, but I thought I might just be lucky here. Am I going to be? Ah. That sort of hornpipe you perform usually means you've got an inspiration or something.'

'Inspiration?' He laid a hand solemnly on her shoulder. 'Doran, you've been guided. I know the very place. He's not been there long, and unless someone's got on to him already and cleaned him out . . . Come on.'

Doran's car was parked in a nearby alley. Peg directed her out of the harbour area, through and behind the insensitively modernized town, through a district of ethnic food shops and cafés, until, in a shabby little square of Georgian and later houses, he said, 'Stop. Here.'

They were outside what looked like a house let off into flats with a sign in the ground-floor window: K. WEDDERBELL. ANTIQUES AND BRIC-A-BRAC.

'Oho,' said Doran. 'I've never heard of a K. Wedderbell in the trade round here.'

'Oho indeed, and let's hope to God nobody else has.'

The three doorbells were labelled in washed-out ink on pasteboard, as though nobody who lived there really expected callers. Peg tried the bottom one. It was answered after they had waited the best part of two minutes, during which distant coughs could be heard, followed by shuffling footsteps.

The man who opened the door looked like a Phiz illustration to Dickens. Thin and slightly bent, he was shabbily dressed in clothes that would have done credit to a production of *Waiting for Godot*. In his lean face the prominent nose was an ominous shade of purple. He smiled nervously.

'Hi, Ken,' Peg greeted him. 'Brought a friend to see you.'

'Ah.' The voice, as well as the hands, quavered. 'Do come in.' As Peg performed introductions, they were led through a narrow hall into the back of what had been a double drawing room, packed with objects. Doran's eye caught a half-tester bed, a japanned cabinet with its doors invitingly open which shrieked seventeenth century at her, a set of mahogany library steps which led the viewer's gaze upwards to a dim oil portrait of a man in early armour, with a distinct look of Holbein about it. She was too startled to take in the small objects lying about on larger ones: only their quality got through to her.

Ken Wedderbell was obviously not a fit man, from whatever cause. He subsided on to a small and very pretty Regency chair, obscuring the dancing nymph or Muse inlaid in marquetry on the back of it.

'I think Ken here may be able to help you, Doran,' said Peg, 'if you can give him an idea what you want.'

Wedderbell glanced from one to the other of them with faded, red-tinged blue eyes.

'That would be marvellous,' she said, 'only I want to hire, not buy, if that would be . . .'

'Perfectly agreeable.' Wedderbell nodded slowly, several times, like a china Mandarin. 'Perfectly agreeable.'

'Oh, good.' Doran was glad she had no occasion to hire the japanned cabinet. 'It's not so much furniture as things that we need for the plot. A spinning wheel, for instance, and things for the cast to sit on, like joint-stools and a coffer, a dower-chest. Chairs wouldn't do because people didn't sit around in them then.'

'The period being –?' Wedderbell gently prompted.

'Oh, didn't I tell you? Sorry. Henry VIII.' For a moment she thought he hadn't heard her, or gone off into a daydream, the faded eyes fixed on a cobwebbed window.

Then he said, 'I have some old oak downstairs. If you've no objection to cellars.'

'Oh, none at all.' They followed him along the hall, dark and damp, down a twisting flight of stone stairs for which Doran, after all, didn't particularly care, to what had obviously been servants' quarters.

The room was equipped with an Edwardian cooking range, once black-leaded, now lustreless, as though no fire could ever have burned in it. The floor space was entirely taken up by furniture, the sort of furniture one never encountered in the trade. Ancient dressers stood round the walls, *dwydarnau* and *tridarnau*, as Howell would have called them. Except for one wall, which was the shoddy cheaply papered background to one of the finest small refectory tables Doran had ever seen. Oak, seventeenth century – earlier?

'Anything you fancy?' Peg asked.

'Anything I fancy? Most of it.' She shook her head, incredulously. That wasn't what this visit was about. Wedderbell had switched on the light, a poor pale bulb with a paper shade. By its inadequate beam she could see two joint-stools, one very low (that would do for Jack Point to crouch on and tell jokes) one nearly the height of a modern dining chair. She indicated them, and Wedderbell picked his way through the oak forest and brought them over to her.

Wormholes. Old. Just flight-holes. No sign of the fine dust which shows the presence of live worm. Not that it mattered, since she was not buying, but it would be too bad if a leg collapsed when one of the cast was sitting on it.

'And this I think you said you wanted.' From a dark corner Wedderbell dragged something too heavy to be carried in his frail arms. It was a spinning wheel.

It had been a working wheel, once – a wisp of dirty wool clung to its spindle.

'I never realized they'd only got three legs,' observed Peg. 'Sure it hasn't lost one?'

'Quite sure,' Doran answered. 'There had to be room for the operator's feet.'

'I'm afraid it isn't early sixteenth, only nineteenth,' Wedderbell proffered timidly, 'but it might do.'

'It will do perfectly.' Doran turned the wheel, which spun satisfactorily. 'What an extraordinary thing, finding one.'

'There are strange chances in life,' Wedderbell said drily.

'Yes, I'd noticed. Now what about a chest of some kind, that two characters could sit on? Something that would make a nice permanent piece of stage furnishing, because there won't be any set changes.'

He spread his hands, indicating that she should choose.

'Plenty of 'em, aren't there?' commented Peg. 'Meg'd go mad if she could see this lot. She'd pack 'em all with stuff.'

They wove in and out of the furniture, examining anything in the shape of a coffer. The result was disappointing. There were not, in fact, plenty, only five, one painted an unpleasant light brown, another with a padded ottoman seat, an ethnic-looking object with ivory inlays, something decorated with painted flowers. The fifth had a mirror laid on it face downwards.

'Oh dear,' Doran said. 'None of them quite right.'

'Ah. This one is – rather a curiosity.' He removed the mirror and cleared a space for her to kneel in and examine the piece. She beckoned Peg over.

It was a large coffer, all of four feet wide and some two and a half feet deep. Oak – or was it all oak? It seemed patchy in places. The front was covered with carvings, about four inches square, divided up by carved heads in bas-relief of an astonishing variety – gargoyles, monsters, monks, snarling wolves and other animals. At each side was carved a small thin caryatid, part man, part woman, with the tail of a fish.

'Hm.' Doran sat back on her heels. 'Would you call it pussy-cat oak?' that being the trade term for Victorian furniture overcrowded with lions' heads and paws.

'Bit more than pussy-cats there,' Peg replied. 'I'd call it the whole zoo – and some pretty funny attendants.'

Doran saw the faintest of smiles on Wedderbell's face.

'Sorry, Mr Wedderbell, being rude about your piece. But it *is* a curiosity. Fake, of course, very, but not all that old. A hundred years? late nineteenth? But what was it made for? Nobody in their right mind could have wanted it to live with.'

'No. It was, in fact (and this is another strange chance) made for stage use. By a craftsman who earned a good living out of making such "period" pieces for costume plays. His name's forgotten now.'

'Did he go off his trolley in the end?' Peg asked, staring at what seemed to be a mermaid with a moustache.

'Not that I know of. He was perhaps proud of his grotesqueries. To my knowledge, that coffer was used in a production of Henry Irving's – *Cymbeline* in 1896. And in *Rope* in the sixties.'

'Well' – Doran got to her feet – 'it's so splendidly awful that I can't resist it. I'll have it, please, and the spinning wheel and the stools.'

'You wouldn't like my refectory table?' Wedderbell asked wistfully.

Doran swerved her eyes away from its perfect proportions and colour. With a thorough cleaning and regular polishing with beeswax and turpentine, it would . . .

'I'd love it, but I could never bear to bring it back.'

They were upstairs again, Doran getting out her cheque book.

'So how much will the hire fees be, and how much deposit would you like?'

Wedderbell seemed to have gone into his trance state again. She repeated the question. He started.

'How much? Oh. Would twenty pounds be too much?'

'Twenty pounds for all that? Far too little. Do let's be realistic.'

But nothing would budge him from the ridiculous sum, and he refused to take a deposit. Half relieved, half embarrassed, Doran arranged for the items to be collected. It was going to be no light job heaving that monster of a chest, but Howell had some strapping roadies he could summon at will.

'Now tell me.' She and Peg were back in the car. 'What's the matter with that man – is he demented?'

Peg shrugged. 'Depends how you look at it. Like I said, he's not been here long and he's not really a pro, but rumours get about. Buzz is, he was curator at a museum, pretty big one. He had this lust for pretty things, and he kind of took some of 'em into protective custody in his own home. Being a bit clumsy about it, he got found out and sent to jug. Seemed some of the stuff was missing, though he swore he hadn't flogged it.'

'Then what?'

'Had a bad breakdown, went into a bin, in fact. Came out, started dealing, but won't charge proper prices – something to do with his conscience. I don't know who he told all this yarn to, but you can tell he . . .' Peg mimed drinking out of a bottle.

A dark thought was forming in Doran's mind. 'Some of the stuff was missing.' What if the things she had hired were among it? And the others, the perfect table, the japanned cabinet, looked as if they'd never been through the trade. Was she a party to crime?

Rodney said it was a very interesting case of compulsive atonement, and Doran was doing the man a favour in accepting such low terms.

'Isn't it called condoning? or compounding? Anyway, I've got my spinning wheel, so let's hope Max has found a Phoebe who can look as if she knew how to use it.'

Max had been auditioning on the Old Primary School's weary piano, to spare the Bell House drawing room from being continually full of hopeful young amateurs. Doran, calling round to report her triumph, was surprised to find the building locked up. Max was back at the Rose, in his attractive beamed room, using its dressing table as a desk and looking, she thought, distraught.

'You've finished auditioning for today, then?'

He glowered. His heavy eyebrows were well designed for glowering.

'I've finished auditioning, period. That's it.'

'Oh.' Doran sat down on a chair completely covered by Max's clothes. They looked as though being sat on wouldn't make them any more rumpled than they were already. 'Well, I hope you've found a good Phoebe, because I've found the most lovely spinning wheel – '

The glower deepened.

'I've engaged the best Phoebe you'll ever see – my own wife.'

'Your . . . But Amy's a pro, isn't she?'

'Aye, she is. Don't worry, you'll not be paying her. I've got her out of a job in Scarborough she wasn't keen on. Her agent's bawling me out, but it's none of his business if she does a charity act for free. That gaggle of ninnies I've had to listen to, cheeping and squawking through "Were I thy Bride . . ." Not one of 'em even fit for chorus work. So I'd no choice.'

'I see.' Doran was disconcerted. 'In that case, what about Elsie? She's a more important character – I mean . . .'

'Elsie Maynard,' said Max, looking Doran defiantly in the eye, 'will be Mrs Paula French. Now I know what you're going to say, you can't stand the bitch, and nor can I. But she's got the nearest thing to a soprano voice I've heard in this bunch, and as she says she can look twenty-three she's going to look it, if it kills both of us. I can see you don't like it, Doran, but there it is.'

'How did she persuade you?'

The eyebrows shot up. Something in Max's outraged expression was not altogether convincing. Doran waited.

'Well. She apologized for her behaviour at the audition. Said it was over-reaction on her part to being thought too old. But her husband had told her afterwards how rude she'd been, and when she heard it put like that she was ashamed of herself.'

'And you believed that?'

'Of course. I still don't take to the woman, and I never shall, but she'll not be so free with her language again.'

'Good,' said Doran. There are various methods of getting one's own way, she reflected, and I've just heard one. She went home to break the bad news to Rodney.

Outside the gate of Bell House a small car was parked. It bore a new registration number and no sign of hard wear. It was a particularly distinguished shade of maroon, like an old-fashioned pram. It had cost more thousands than Doran cared to think about. It could only belong to one person she knew.

In the hall, even before she opened the kitchen door, a subtle but pervasive Italian perfume told her who was on the other side of it.

She ran forward with a cry of welcome.

'Tiggy!'

4

A merrymaid peerly proud

Tiggy Denshaw and Doran had first met at a very superior country-house hotel, Caxton Manor, where Doran had been involved in two murders tied up with the antique trade, and Tiggy had been one of the very young, Victorian-garbed waitresses, multi-skilled and faultlessly educated.

Since then a friendship had grown up between them. Doran staying at Tiggy's flat in London when she needed an overnight stop. She was not over-blessed with friends in Abbotsbourne, and found Tiggy's bright youth, dazzling prettiness and lively conversation a refreshing change. They went out to dinner together at fun places, Tiggy had spent a quick weekend or two at Bell House. Doran hoped this was to be another of them.

'Doran, but how totally wondrous to see you.' Tiggy put her arms round Doran in the lightest, most fragrant of embraces. She was a delight to the eye, the apparition of an angel in that familiar kitchen. Her long, straight, shining hair's russet had been delicately gold-tinted to the brightness of a new wedding-ring, the childish purity of her skin needed no make-up, her large eyes beamed with the sweetness of good nature. She was one of the few people Doran knew who made you feel that while you were with her you were the only person who mattered in her world.

Her real name was Victoria. She had only the vaguest idea how she had come to be known as Tiggy – something to do with a nanny who read Beatrix Potter to her, she thought, and subsequent befriendings by her of numerous hedgehogs at her father's Sussex country house. Tiggywinkles, of course. Her mother, Lady Mary, had sympathized with her daughter's concern for orphaned hedgehog babies, but forbidden their presence in the house because of their overpowering stench. But Tiggy herself had loved them too much to notice it, or their fleas.

'I was just passing through Abbotsbourne, acksherley,' Tiggy said, 'because my job had finished, they've gone to their place in Minorca for the summer, and I thought I'd have a breath of air with Nan in Brighton.' Nan was Tiggy's maternal grandmother, who looked a fairly young forty and lived in a Regency villa high above the sea. 'Then I thought I'd go off course a bit and look in on you all. If you don't mind.'

'Mind! We're enchanted. Aren't we, Rodney.'

Rodney appeared to be in exactly that state. Standing by the kitchen table, a cheese-grater in one hand and a piece of Double Gloucester in the other, he was staring at Tiggy as though moonstruck.

'Yes,' he managed to say. 'Yes, we are. Enchanted.'

'Let me do that.' Tiggy took the cheese and grater from him, reached down a clean plate, and briskly began to shred the cheese on to it. 'How much? Omelette? Sauce au gratin?'

'Just – er – Welsh rarebit for Kit's tea,' replied Kit's father.

'Oh, my precious Kit. Where is he? Has he grown a lot since Christmas? Oh, I do want to see him – you wouldn't believe the two little ghastlies I've been nannying, twins, but they utterly hated each other, the boy had a voice like a gravel-mixer and the girl wasn't awfully well trained and enjoyed not being, if you know what I mean. Where's the bread? You need a drop of beer with the cheese if Kit's allowed to have it.'

'Ah. Beer . . .' Rodney glanced round as if expecting elfin hands to produce a bottle out of the wall.

'In the fridge, of course, and yes, Tiggy, he is allowed to have a touch of alcohol now and again, on the French principle.' Doran was remembering the wonderful meals she'd had at Tiggy's flat, for Tiggy had gone through a cordon bleu course of cookery, not to mention a few things she had picked up from her Swiss finishing school and holidays abroad. She was also bi-lingual in French and German, had been convent-trained to sew exquisitely, and was a qualified nanny who adored children, whatever she may have said about her past charges. A Sloane char, a dozen domestics rolled into one, and a friend . . .

Doran was surprised to hear her own voice daring to ask, 'Tiggy – could you possibly stay? With us, I mean, instead of Nan? We do need you so awfully. It's mean to take advantage, when you need a holiday, and you may loathe the idea, but you see . . .'

Tiggy listened to the story of the *Yeomen* production, of the defection of Kit's ex-nanny, of Vi's being pushed to the limit, having to be at Bell House so much when she had other jobs to do as well, of Rodney's being needed every evening at future rehearsals – 'and though I'm not a performer I shall have to be *there*, stage-managing . . .'

Of course a tired, overworked au pair wouldn't want to know about filling in domestically on her first holiday of the year. It had been brash, unforgivable to ask, when Tiggy had only dropped in to say hello on her way to Brighton.

Tiggy smiled, the smile of a Bernini marble angel.

'I didn't dare hope you'd ask me. Because I want to, so much.'

'I've solved the costume problem,' Rodney said complacently.

Doran, coming downstairs from putting Kit to bed, laid a finger against her lips. 'Ssh. Tiggy told him a bedtime story, and it seemed to hypnotize him – he fell asleep instantly as soon as she stopped, quite unlike him.'

'Good. I said I've solved your costume problem.'

'You've – what? I don't believe you. How?'

'Simon Peasmarsh.'

'Who . . . Oh, him. The martyr.'

'That's right. The Barminster Martyr, burned by Mary Tudor in 1555 after leading a local revolt against her. They celebrate him every September, on the anniversary, with a play done in Cloister Garth. *And* they keep the costumes for it in a room off the ringing chamber in the cathedral. So!'

'But,' said the pedantic Doran, 'isn't that a bit late for Henry VIII costumes?'

'Not in the slightest. Eight years – and I'd bet the fashions didn't change much in those days, especially not with a boy king in between. They were probably still wearing their grandparents' clothes, in any case.'

'But how would we get the costumes? If they're any good, that is.'

'Hire them. And slip a small something into the collection box. If I understand old Canon Porter aright, and he's so deaf I doubt if he really understood *me* on the phone, that's the way to do it. We can go and see them tomorrow – I've arranged to pick up the key.'

'How wonderful! You're very clever indeed.' She kissed his cheek.

'*I've wisdom from the East and from the West, That's subject to no academic rule.*' Rodney executed a Point-like *pas seul* down the hall.

Doran marvelled. It was the first time she had seen him identify at all with the character he had said he wanted to perform. Yet now Jack Point had, quite suddenly, come alive. She heard him singing in the kitchen, and followed him.

'You needn't bother to peel vegetables,' she told him, 'though it was a kindly thought. Tiggy's offered to make dinner for us all. Now won't that be a treat!'

Rodney bent down and stroked the cat Tybalt, who was asleep on a chair and unresponsive to caresses. His face was turned away from Doran as he said, 'Yes. It would indeed be a treat.'

The costumes at Barminster were better than anyone could have expected. They were crowded so thickly on their rails in the little room off the cathedral's ringing chamber that Doran, Max and Meg (who had been appointed wardrobe adviser) had to drag them out into the chamber itself, which was well lit by a large stained-glass window and two plain-leaded ones.

Rodney said the atmosphere was too stuffy for him, and went down to look at his favourite monuments. To Meg the old-clo' miasma was home from home.

'Been cleaned and pressed every time they've been used,' she pronounced. 'Kept mended, too. Hems have been up and down, we'll just fit them to height. Good thing ruffs weren't in by this period, or we'd have all that starching to do.'

They surveyed kirtles and farthingales, bodices, aprons, hoods, doublets and hose ('We'll have to use ordinary tights, these are much too baggy,' Doran said) and a selection of what could only be described as peasant gear.

Max thought the costumes too drab. 'We'll want colour, not all these browns and sludges.'

'Then we'll put some in,' Doran said. 'We'll scrap those nothing-colour aprons and crossover bits and use our own. I've lots left over from the last jumble sale. We can always dye things – ours, not theirs.'

'Brilliant. I've got some shawls . . .' Meg was counting on her fingers. 'A red one for that skirt, bright blue for this . . .'

'Just one wee detail.' Max's voice was dry. 'I don't see any uniforms for the Yeomen themselves.'

A silence fell, as they pictured the gold-emblazoned scarlet knee-length Tudor coats and breeches, the ruffs (for after all there *were* ruffs), the round-brimmed black hats . . .

'I couldn't make all those,' Meg said glumly. 'And the material would cost a packet. We can't do it.'

'No. Oh dear. What fools we were not to have thought of it.'

Max's wintry smile appeared. 'I know a man who . . .'

'Yes?' they chorused.

'Never mind. I'll fix it – I think.'

Doran sighed with relief. 'You're a wonderful being, Max. Oh look! that doublet's perfect for Shadbolt, with the nasty-looking buckle on the belt. And that coif for Dame Carruthers . . .' She paused. 'I've just noticed something.'

Meg groaned.

'There's no jester's costume for Jack Point. Well, there wouldn't be, would there, in a play about the burning of a local martyr? Unless some visiting nobleman had brought his Fool along to watch the fun, which wouldn't have looked very well from the front. We'll just have to make one, that's all – sew little bells on to one of these doublets and – '

'No need,' said a voice behind them. It was Rodney, returned. 'Point needn't make his entrance in jester's costume.'

'*What?*'

'He'd been kicked out of his last job – for telling a bishop a joke that was too French, if I remember rightly – and he wouldn't have been allowed to keep his livery, only his fool's bauble, the stick with a clown's head on it. So he simply enters in Act One in ordinary doublet and hose and wearing, as they used to say, his own hair.'

They considered this novel suggestion, Doran with especial thought. Point's traditional belled hood concealed all the hair, leaving only the face visible. Rodney's thick, curling brown hair, with its becoming sprinkle of grey, would never be seen by the audience. Point's traditional knee-length, dagged-hem jerkin was foreshortening to a man's figure, nor were parti-coloured hose flattering to long, graceful, muscular legs.

Rodney didn't care about looking funny. He wanted to look nice.

How odd, and quaint, and just a shade pathetic. Doran took his hand and held it, to convey solidarity.

'Oh no he doesn't.' Max's voice was loud enough to have started the cathedral bells ringing, harnessed though they were by their tied sallies. 'Not in any production of mine, Point doesn't bloody enter in doublet and hose. Who's going to know who he is? Look like a poof, wouldn't he?'

'Not necessarily,' replied Rodney stiffly.

'I do think Max is right,' put in Meg. 'It's the costume makes the man, really, isn't it?'

'I rather thought the performance made the man,' Rodney said.

Doran squeezed his hand and murmured, 'No use arguing, he's made his mind up.'

Rodney pulled his hand away. 'Very well, if that's the way you want it. *There are one or two rules That all family fools must observe if they love their profession*. Case in point. Sorry, no jokes intended.'

But Doran knew he was not pleased to have lost the argument.

The first read-through was on stage at the Old Primary School, where the performance itself was to be held. It was a close runner-up for the title of ugliest building in Elvesham, belonging to the 1880s with bricks of a repulsive red and an interior of gloomy austerity, retaining memories of temperance rallies, local council elections, and jumble sales held indoors because of rain. Its pervading atmosphere came from either drains or dry rot. Doran made mental lists – air purifiers, sprays, a firm policy of open doors in the daytime.

Max dropped the first bomb with his announcement that it was to be a sing-through as well as a read-through. A general groan went up. He ignored it, handing round a pile of scores. He seated himself at the piano, a new hired one which had replaced the rattling old upright.

'Now, if you can sight-read, do it. If not just say the words to the tune, as I play it. For now. In a fortnight I want ye word-perfect and note-perfect. Okay? Right. Phoebe.'

Because Amy wasn't yet available, Doran had been given Phoebe to read. It was just her luck that the part began with a song. Phoebe musing on love at her spinning wheel. '*When maiden loves*' had probably never been worse rendered. She recalled singing a random selection of Sullivan songs while imprisoned in a church vault, on one of her rash adventures. They'd sounded all right, then. Perhaps entombment improved the voice.

Max stopped her after the first verse.

'Okay. Just do the reading. Shadbolt and Phoebe.'

They did the reading. Simon was quite awful. No head jailer in the history of the prison industry had ever spoken with such a lofty accent. Ruth glanced at him reproachfully. Somebody giggled, and Max tapped his foot with undisguised impatience.

'Right, cut the Chorus. Dame Carruthers. You – Guy – read Second Yeoman.'

Quivering with nerves Guy got through the lines,

Ruth replying in her fine strong voice. When Max started the Prelude to 'When our gallant Norman foes' she straightened her back, flashed her eyes, and went confidently into the grim words and their *alla marcia* setting.

'*The screw may twist and the rack may turn,*
And men may bleed and men may burn,
O'er London town and its golden hoard
I keep my silent watch and ward.'

There was a scatter of applause, then they stumbled on, Guy gaining visible confidence, as though he sensed Doran willing him to improve, though it was to Paula that his eyes went.

Enter Colonel Fairfax, guarded. Rupert Wylie, loud-voiced, hamming up the dialogue, doing the full Victorian tenor act.

'Look, shall I sing "*Is Life a boon*"?'

He did. He was not half bad, though he gave far too much weight to the delicate lyric. He would look magnificent in the splendid costume Meg had found for him, a velvet doublet of dark gold, with trunk-hose of emerald green. More magnificent than he deserved, Doran thought. On they went, to the entrance of Point and Elsie.

Doran, though reasonably prepared, was startled to hear just how much the spirit of the wandering jester had taken over her husband. He was reading his lines, but made them sound as if they had only just come from his brain. A witty, frightened man, using his wit to turn a hostile crowd's jeers to amusement. He and Elsie will sing for them, dance for them.

Elsie spoke. 'Let us give them the singing farce of the Merryman and his Maid – therein is song and dance too.' Loud, confident: and she'd memorized the words.

Rodney half sang the first line of that duet which is anything but a farce. '*I have a song to sing, O!*'

'*Sing me your song, O!*'

Paula's answer came back at him like the hearty soprano bellow of a Principal Boy inviting her audience to join in the chorus. Max visibly jumped, Doran tried not to look at Rodney.

She was word-perfect. The tale of the jilted merry-maid who went back to her moping merryman and begged on her knees for his love, came across loud and clear, almost deafening in the acoustics of the bare building.

Max opened his mouth and shut it again, tightly. Euan threw his wife a look of glowing admiration. Guy was gazing raptly at her, Rupert was grinning. The read-through wore on, the cast stumbling through the lines, sometimes turning two pages over at once, sometimes getting the sense wrong. Never had the humour seemed so flat, the plot so unconvincing. Only Rodney kept in character, up till the last moment, when Point realizes that he has lost his girl to her bridegroom, Fairfax.

'*He sipped no sup and he craved no crumb*
As he sighed for the love of a ladye . . .'

His breath seemed to give out. He slipped from the chair to his knees, crawled across the floor to Paula's feet, caught at the hem of her dress and kissed it, made the sign of the Cross in the air, and fell prone.

There were gasps, a cry from Paula. Doran managed to restrain herself from going to Rodney just before he calmly got to his feet and resumed his seat.

Max said, 'It's past eleven, we've been at this over three hours. I'm bushed and I'm sure you all are. I shan't give any notes now, but I can tell you there'll have to be some cuts, a lot. I advise every one of you to read the libretto for yourselves at home and make sure ye understand it. Just for a start. Good night.'

As he reached the door Paula called after him, 'I

know my part perfectly well, Max. In fact, I've got some ideas you might like to – '

'Not now, thanks.' The door slammed behind him.

In the car Doran said, 'You frightened me. I thought you'd fainted. Or even . . . Though I knew you hadn't, really.'

'No, I hadn't. I was doing the same business as Henry Lytton. He played Point in D'Oyly Carte's company when nobody knew what Gilbert meant at the end. He decided to die of a heart attack. It worked, Elsie burst into tears every night and Carte loved it.'

'Your Elsie didn't burst into tears. She saw herself being out-acted – she was furious. Oh, Rodney, how frightful she is! And yet she *can* sing.'

'They're all frightful. Even Ruth sounds like a contralto frog. And there was a bad feeling in the room. That's why I made the Sign.'

'I thought it was.'

'You know,' Rodney added, driving through the gate of Bell House, thoughtfully opened by someone, 'there's a great deal about death in *The Yeomen. From the dungeon to the block, from the scaffold to the grave . . .*'

'That's right. *And the funeral bell tolling, tolling Bim-a-boom . . .* You don't suppose this is one of *those* pieces – like the Scotch Play? You know, doomy, dangerous to put on?'

'I've never heard anything of the kind. Look, there's a light in the kitchen. Tiggy's still up.'

Tiggy was not only up, she had laid out a delicious light supper with a bottle of exactly the right wine and tea or coffee for whoever wanted them. Kit had demanded *Peter Rabbit* twice, then gone immediately to sleep.

Doran kissed her. 'You're wonderful.'

Tiggy, her newly washed hair shining on the shoulders of her gauzy blue negligée, beamed. 'I thought the evening might have been a bit trying.'

'It was,' Rodney said, 'until now.'

His eyes were saying more. Doran remembered Point kissing the hem of Elsie's dress. Rodney must be still living the part, how sweet.

5

Dark danger hangs upon the deed

It had been a frantic week, one way or another. The production was to be in three weeks' time, on a Saturday matinée and evening, a very short space for the drilling of so many people who had only the faintest idea what they were doing.

At least some things went right. Doran, as stage manager and Props, was given some problem objects to find. A block and an axe for the beheading, for instance.

'But nobody gets beheaded, because Fairfax escapes,' she reasoned. 'Can't we just imagine it?'

Max's answer was patient, pitying.

'It's only the best curtain in all the works of G. and S., isn't it? The Headsman standing there masked, with his chopper at the ready, on the darkening stage, with Elsie falling in a faint and the music going . . .' He demonstrated how the music went. 'You want that scene played without the block?'

'Well, no. Oh dear. I'll ask Annabella.'

Annabella Firle, serious, sensible, her early beauty subjugated now by enormous spectacles, responded cheeringly.

'Easy. A grocer's box, cut along the sides so they can lean inward, the top replaced by the hollow bit where the head goes – that would be papier-mâché – all painted black, and weighted with sand so that it won't get kicked about.'

Doran marvelled. 'Simple. I never thought of that – only that the Tower wouldn't be too avid to lend us theirs. What about the axe, though? We've got a chopper in the woodshed – do you think that would do?'

'Not impressive enough. And a cardboard one would just look silly.'

Jack Turner the pork butcher, who had no singing voice and tended to hover purposelessly at rehearsal, came up with the solution.

'I use choppers, don't I? What you want is a good long-handled 'un as'll show. I want my bit to be good,' he added proudly.

The weapon he produced from his shop was certainly impressive. Its handle was nearly three feet long, and its blade the sinister shape familiar from illustrations of execution scenes. It was, he said, just an old one they didn't use. The women shuddered at it, all but Paula, who touched it with one pearly nail.

'No edge at all. Why don't you put some silver paint on it, to catch the light?'

'Because I say not,' snapped Max. She shrugged. He was very unresponsive to her suggestions for improving his production, ungrateful man.

Doran's other properties were more difficult. Rodney said he needed a copy of *The Merrie Jestes of Hugh Ambrose*. 'Point says, "*Ah! 'Tis but melancholy mumming when poor heart-broken jilted Jack Point must needs turn to Hugh Ambrose for original light humour.*" The audience need to see where he gets his awful cracks from.'

'Then get one.'

'Not easy, Max,' Doran said. 'It was never written, unfortunately. Just one of Gilbert's own Merrie Jestes.'

'How do you know that?' Rodney inquired.

'It's one of the footnotes in our copy. Unlike you not to have read a footnote. In any case, it would be no use having an ordinary-sized book on stage, there's nothing funny about that. It needs to be an outsize thing – anyone got a spare First Folio they wouldn't mind lending? Only joking. Back to Annabella, then.'

Annabella just happened to know of an enormous, but flattish *Illustrated London News* for 1887 in her father's possession. Within two hours of finding it she had transformed it with a brown paper jacket, suitably aged in appearance, hand-printed with the title in black and scarlet, and a drawing of a nodding fool's head.

'Sometimes I despair,' Doran said. 'Why call me a stage manager? I'm nothing but a person who stands about not knowing the answers. Like, for instance, how I can produce a big enough bunch of keys for Shadbolt, on the same principle.'

'A very large wire ring would do it,' Annabella suggested, 'with a lot of fairly big keys on it. Like the church key – and the one for the Old Primary School.'

'I did know, of course, Rodney's got them both. At least I don't have to do anything about the costume fittings. Nobody will like what they get and it'll have nothing to do with me.'

Nobody did like what they got, and it was quite extraordinary how at the trying-on session few costumes fitted anybody, particularly the twelve Yeomen suits Max had somehow conjured up. Rodney's motley had not yet been put together by Meg, but he had found himself a doublet and hose which were remarkably becoming. Doran, who had never seen him in any kind of costume before, unless one counted canonicals, thought it made him look like an attractive, slightly disturbing ghost of himself.

'Elsie! Where's Paula?' Meg, holding the Elsie costume on its hanger, looked round the Old Primary School, milling with discontented people.

'She's not here.'

'She'll be here in a minute.' This was Euan, struggling with the buttons of First Citizen. 'She had something special to do.'

As he spoke, Paula came in, not at all flustered,

Doran noticed. She was wearing a light raincoat which covered her from neck to knee.

'Oh *do* come on, Paula.' Meg waved the costume, which she had pinned loosely together – green calf-length skirt, black laced corselet, white cotton blouse. 'We've tried nearly everybody's but yours. I *think* it'll fit, but I can always add a band of one of the colours to the hem – '

'Darling Meg' – Paula bestowed a light kiss in passing on Meg's cheek – 'how sweet of you. *À la gitane* – gypsy style, as it's usually known. Very quaint. They used to dress Elsie like that up to the 1948 revival, didn't they? A bit tacky and quaint now, don't you think? And after all why should Elsie be a gypsy? Maynard isn't exactly a Romany name. I feel it's time we got back to the historical reality, don't you?'

She let the raincoat fall. Beneath it she wore a dress of scarlet, cut in early Tudor style, the bell skirts short to the ankle for dancing. A delicate pleated net frill bordered the low-plunging square neckline, and the waist was emphasized with a line of gilt needlework. Otherwise the material was ornamented only – only! – by hundreds of multi-coloured sequins, glittering and flashing points of fire. On her short, boyish hair she perched a delicious little Tudor cap, with a mock jewel and a feather in it.

Guy uttered a stifled cry, half-rising in his seat, hands outstretched. Faust seeing the vision of Helen of Troy, thought Doran. Maggie pulled him down.

Meg's voice topped the chorus of oohs and ahhs in a rising squeak.

'You can't wear that!'

'Oh? Why not?'

'Because it'd make everybody else look what you call tacky and quaint, that's why not. That's a ballet dress. And it's hand-made.'

'Yes, Paula sat up two nights making it,' chimed in Euan. Paula threw him a you-shut-up glare.

'I ran it up myself, certainly. Any objection?'

Meg snatched up her jacket and stumped out, not even shutting the door. They heard her car start up and go roaring off.

The costume-fitting broke up in disorder.

'That *woman*!' Ruth burst out to Doran. 'She's outrageous! The sheer brazen cheek of it. She can't get away with it, can she?'

'Of course not. Max will stop her.'

Max was too taken up with the arrival of his wife Amy to listen to horror stories until Amy had been thoroughly introduced to everyone. Doran liked her on sight. She was a sweet-faced, slightly too plump woman, as theatrical as grease-paint and as anxious to please as her name suggested. She was also deeply superstitious, beyond the usual for her profession. She seized on the châtelaine of antique silver household objects Doran wore round her waist.

'Oh, my dear! there's something tremendously lucky on this. I do wonder what . . .'

'Try it on.'

The châtelaine was a tight fit for Amy's curves. She fingered the objects on it, circumventing the swell of her bosom and hips.

'It's not the scissors. Or the thimble. Perhaps it's . . . yes, it's the fish.' She turned her charm full on at Doran, and it was real charm, a childlike winningness.

'Could I borrow it? To wear with my costume, I mean? Phoebe *would* wear a châtelaine, wouldn't she, she was a domesticated sort of girl, keeping house for her father, well, I suppose she did, though Dame Carruthers might have done that as well as housekeep for the Tower . . . oh, anyway, please can I borrow it? I can see it's valuable but I'll guard it with my life, I promise.'

'It's insured. Yes, of course you can. Only not to rehearsals, if you don't mind. The other costumes are mostly not ready, because we're having a little difficulty. Speaking of which, Max . . .' She told him.

Max erupted. He went on erupting until Paula herself arrived. She was wearing the scarlet dress.

'Take yon rag off.' His tone was grim.

'Oh, but it does something for me, takes me straight into the part.'

'Ye'll not be singing the part. Ye're fired.'

'You can't fire me. You haven't time to get anyone else.'

Max took a deep, power-charging breath. Then he loosed a flood of invective, some of it new to Doran, in an accent which slid downwards into the voice and language of his origins, Port Glasgow.

Translated, it informed Paula that she sang like a female cat in the final throes of sexual tension, that her effrontery in giving him advice about his production was something he had never encountered during twenty-five years in the theatre (and included the dress which would have done nicely if the character-list had included a Tudor whore) and finally, with some touches recalled from his days in the Navy, he reasserted his belief that she was years too old for the part.

Paula went a strange, livid colour, as though about to be sick.

Amy trilled, 'Max, darling! really . . .'

Rodney said, 'We won't have women spoken to like that here, Max.'

Euan put his arms round his wife and glared. 'Come on, pet. We're going home.' She shrugged him off, as though brushing a wasp away.

It was Guy who went up to Max and hit him on the chin, starting a fight in which Maggie joined, trying to pull her brother away and getting blows herself in the attempt. A girl screamed and somebody said, 'Phone the police.'

Rodney shouted above all the commotion, 'Stop it!'

Like a film slowing down, the three entangled figures parted. Guy was on his knees, rising painfully to his feet and rubbing his shoulder. His nose was bleeding. Max had a cut at the corner of his mouth. Guy approached Euan, shaking a damaged fist.

'What sort of a husband are you then, blast you? Leaving it to outsiders to defend your wife against that foul-mouthed – berk. Not a man at all, by the looks of you, just a poncing gay that fancies being married to the most – '

'Out,' commanded Rodney. At a glance from him Ruth opened the door and stood by it.

'Take Paula home, Euan,' he said. 'You others, calm down a bit, then go off home yourselves. That's enough for one evening. Sorry to take over, Max, but you went too far.'

'Yes, you did, love,' Amy said, dabbing at Max's cheek with a handkerchief. 'They're not used to naughty words like that. It'll all be forgotten by the time we start again tomorrow.'

'Will it?' Rupert Wylie caught up with Doran as she went to the car.

'I shouldn't think so. I didn't notice you leaping to Paula's defence, by the way.'

He laughed, his loudest rugger-story laugh.

'That old lady? Why should I? Now if it had been you . . .'

'Oh, do shut up, Rupert, I'm not in the mood.'

'When will you be?'

'Never.'

Rupert suddenly took her by the shoulders and pinned her against a tree on the road's verge. 'In that case, give us a kiss.'

She struggled briefly with him before escaping to her car. It seemed an evening for struggling.

'Oh, no,' Doran said to herself. The driver's window of her car had been wound down only a very little, but enough to allow a wasp in. By this time, imprisoned, it was very angry. Impossible to drive off with it as a companion. She tried shooing, prodding at it with a newspaper, everything but the one sure way she knew to trap wasps, which was with a beer-baited jam jar, not practicable at the moment.

It was not interested in being lured or sworn at, only in expressing his rage. Baffled, Doran left all four doors wide and stood away from the car to consider strategy.

The wasp emerged and flew swiftly away, muttering. Or that was how it sounded.

In the silence and calm she wiped her hot face and breathed deeply.

Not quite silence. From somewhere out of sight, probably behind the trees that hid the school entrance, voices came, a young female one, as indignant as the wasp's.

'Leave me alone! Of course I won't. Don't be silly. Are you drunk or something?'

The reply was inaudible, but the laugh was unmistakable – Rupert's.

Sex-mad, Doran said to herself. Perhaps he's got satyriasis. I wonder if he'll grow cloven hooves eventually? And who can it be this time? Not Meg, surely.

Her question was answered by the appearance of a young woman, at speed, emerging from the school gate and running towards a parked car. It was Annabella.

Doran got into her car and started it. How, she wondered, would the translation of feet into hooves affect such matters as buying socks and shoes? Annabella, of all girls, so young, so – well, plain. At least in her present stage of growth. They must be all one to Rupert, so long as they're female . . .

On the stage, about to leave, with Rodney, Ruth and the muttering Max behind her, Amy caught sight of the property furniture huddled in a corner.

'Oh, look – they've got me a spinning wheel! How marvellous.'

'Do you know how to work it?' Ruth asked. 'Because there's a woman in the village who could show you.'

'No need. I used one in *Faust*, I used to sit spinning away. Faust sees Gretchen in the vision, you know . . . oh, I must try it.'

She perched herself on the small joint-stool and began to rotate the wheel. After three turns she stopped with a faint shriek.

'Oh! it's bad. I feel it. Something bad's happened connected with this thing.' She jumped up. 'I can't use it, I won't. They must find me another.'

'Doran was very pleased to have found that one,' Ruth said sharply. She had been deeply shocked by Max's language to Paula, and was not disposed to humour his wife's whims. 'I don't think we can ask her to change it.'

'Just one of Amy's wee humours,' Max murmured. 'She gets these psychic notions.' To Amy he said, 'Don't fret, dearie.'

Rodney let himself into Bell House. A far-off murmur of song led him to the drawing room. One standard lamp shed a soft light over it. Outside the French windows the garden glimmered through the evening gloom. Tiggy sat in a long chair by the window. She was wearing something gauzy and flowing, and Kit was in her arms, fast asleep, his head thrown back against her shoulder. It was a scene, Rodney felt, from an Edwardian painting: *Twilight Thoughts*. She could have been a visiting spirit, the child's angel.

She looked up, smiling, and switched on a reading lamp beside her.

'Hello. What sort of evening did you have?'

'Nasty, brutish and short, as Hobbes remarked. Let's not discuss it. What's the old boy doing up this late?'

She stroked Kit's hair back from his sleeping brow. 'He had a touch of ear-ache, poor chap. The stuff in the bathroom cupboard stopped it, but he still wanted a bit of nursing, so . . .'

Lucy Kit. Fortunate child. A man wouldn't mind being four again and having a touch of ear-ache for that sort of treatment.

'If you'll take him, I think he'll stay asleep,' she said, 'and I can get you a drink.'

'No, just stay where you are,' Rodney sat down, firmly choosing a seat at the opposite side of the room. '*What a helpless ninny is a love-sick man*,' he mused. '*He is but as a lute in a woman's hands . . .*'

'Sorry? I didn't hear what you said.'

'Just rehearsing.' Someone else's lines, but they fitted – all too well.

Doran's car door slammed in the drive. Kit woke and stirred, Rodney said, 'Ah, Doran's back,' and Tiggy gave the faintest of little sighs.

The heat in the schoolroom was sweltering. Through the grimy, high window panes the evening sun streamed from the west, turning each window into a burning-glass, showing up in unpleasant detail the small nests of departed spiders and their mummified webs which took up each corner of each pane.

The cast sweated and shifted chairs, speaking their lines with increasing languor. Necks were mopped with handkerchiefs, at first discreetly, then openly. Frequent trips were made to the tap in the kitchen, though the water it gave was lukewarm and brackish. Max, whose temper was worsening, unbuttoned his shirt to the waist. Rupert took his off completely, revealing a glistening muscular torso. Doran wilted. Rodney looked so pale that he might have been already made up for his collapse at the end of the opera.

Paula had turned up to rehearsal. She must be, Doran decided, unsquashable, not capable of feeling real hurt. Only a totally insensitive person could have taken Max's insults and sprung back into place like a punch-ball. Her vanity was such that no obstacle was too much to keep her from showing herself off in the part she saw as her own: and the force of it overcame Max's resistance, once his fury had blown itself out. She was reinstated with only a token struggle on his part.

She had made her Elsie dress: she was going to wear it, if it killed her. Ever prepared, she produced a stick of iced cologne and applied it fragrantly to her temples and wrists, offering it to the other women very much as an after-thought, then reclaiming it swiftly before they could pollute it. Then, before putting it away, she leant across Rodney to offer it to Guy, smiling radiantly. He stuttered some sort of thanks, without using it (too sacred? Doran wondered).

'Shut up!' Max bellowed, crashing his hands down on the piano keys. 'Is it not enough trying to work in this hellish dump? Do I have to have twittering and cheeping going on like a nest of blasted sparrows?'

Guy went even more scarlet than he was.

Paula said sharply, '*I* wasn't twittering or cheeping, and if Guy twittered or cheeped it was only by way of politeness.'

Max threw her a glance of hatred. 'I didn't ask for comments, I said Shut Up.'

Doran had been thinking as she looked out through the open back door into the garden.

'I wonder,' she ventured with a Miss Marple cough,

'if I could make a suggestion. Could we possibly rehearse outside? It really is like the Burning Fiery Furnace in here, and there's a good big patch of grass out there, room for all of us, I should think.'

Max pondered. 'Traffic noise, And we need the piano.'

'There isn't any traffic noise apart from the odd car, and the piano's on wheels.'

Max's creased face relaxed into something like a smile.

'Okay with me if everyone else agrees,' he said.

Amy jumped up with a theatrical cry of relief and gave him a sticky kiss, as the rest of them, echoing her, pushed their chairs back and surged outside.

'Good thinking.' Rodney touched Doran's shoulder. 'I was beginning to identify utterly with Shadrach, Meshach and Abednego, and the Angel seemed to be running late.'

Outside everybody puffed and gasped in the relatively fresh air. What had been a playground was now grassed and surrounded by a neglected flower border. It was far from picturesque, but it lay in the shadow of the school, out of the eye of the westering sun, and was blissfully cool after the interior.

'*O Paradise, O Paradise, 'tis weary waiting here.* Or rather it was weary waiting there,' Rodney said.

'I don't want to interfere with Paradise, but Max wants you as a removal man.'

They joined in the task of shifting chairs to the lawn, the men manoeuvring the piano, so fortunately on castors, down the single step into the garden. Paula managed to move only her chair, which she promptly sat on, fanning herself.

'Oh dear,' she said to Ruth, who had taken the next chair, 'I do hope the light isn't too strong out here. One can get sunburnt from reflected rays, you know.'

'Can one? I never have.'

'Ah, but you're dark. At least, you were, weren't you.'

Ruth bridled, and began to answer, but checked herself. What was the use, with one to whom bitchery came so naturally? It would only make her hotter to answer back.

'I wish I had my hat,' Paula breathed wistfully. 'My little Tudor hat. I *could* go back in and fetch it. Oh, but it hasn't really any brim.'

Doran was dreamy, almost asleep, when the last of the sunset went off the ox-blood bricks of the Old Primary School, and evening shadows began to dim the surroundings and the faces of the cast. They were working through to the end of Act One. Guy had made an unconvincingly nervous entrance as Leonard Meryll, returning to the Tower after a career of knightly valour, and now Rupert was making another entrance, Colonel Fairfax disguised as Leonard, swaggering, mock-modest, declaring that '*the tales that of his prowess were narrated Had been prodigiously exaggerated*'.

Nobody would believe that for a minute, of course. He looked capable of tackling a regiment or a team of Black Belts, with those muscles. What a pity he wasn't in costume yet. And what a pity the costume didn't feature a codpiece, as some Tudor ones did: how Rupert would have enjoyed that.

Now he was greeting his supposed sister, Phoebe Meryll, and being warned by her jealous suitor, the jailer Shadbolt, that Phoebe was a touch too free with her affections and in need of brotherly supervision.

'*And when she feels (as sometimes she does feel)*
Disposed to indiscriminate caress,
Be thou at hand to take those favours from her!'

What an extraordinary piece of advice to be in a Victorian opera, if one followed it to its logical conclusion...

And, speaking of indiscriminate caresses, Doran was aware of someone present who was more than ready for them: a sweat-shiny young sultan, hot-eyed, stripped to the waist, Rupert under the influence of a summer night. The last verse of his duet with Phoebe required a kiss at the end of each line. The kisses seemed to be taking as long as the lines, and there was a backward movement of Amy's shoulders, as though she were trying to get away.

Max, busy playing the lively accompaniment, had his eyes on the score. But everybody else watched the duettists, fascinated.

'From dim twilight to 'leven at night
That compact I will seal.'

sang Rupert, before enfolding the tiny Amy in a swamping embrace.

A few people clapped, someone cheered. Max half turned, saw nothing but two singers moving apart.

'Cue bell,' he said. 'Bell? Where's the bell?'

'Sorry.' Doran came to herself. 'I forgot — the props are all inside.'

'Okay. Imagine bell. Chorus, *The prisoner comes to meet his doom.*'

'Er. We can't have a chorus rehearsal till Monday,' Doran ventured (as if he didn't know that already). 'Is it any use going on to the end, Max?'

'Walk it, walk it.' He struck the chord of the solemn funeral march for Fairfax. Amy was back in her chair, her face very flushed, scrubbing her mouth with her handkerchief.

After the curtain music there was a gathering up of chairs and music, and a general exodus towards homes or pubs. Doran was one of the last to leave. She noticed a bunch of keys still sticking in the main door of the school — Rodney, who was responsible for them, must have forgotten to lock up. He was very absent-minded these days. She would do it herself and take them to him in the car.

Someone was still in the garden: two people, Max and Amy. Max was very angry, his words inaudible, but the tone unmistakable. Amy was sobbing. Oh dear, then Max had been told about the duet.

'I don't really care what happens to Rupert,' she told Rodney as they drove away, 'but it wouldn't help to have a blow-up between him and Max at this stage, would it? Especially as he isn't really after Amy, anyone would do, he's just randy — it's the weather. Oh!'

'What?'

'There he is, and he's got a woman with him. Going up the little path to the wood.'

'Good.' Rodney sounded supremely uninterested. Doran, glancing at his austere, set profile, wondered whether he was losing too much of himself in the part he was playing. Faintly snubbed and hurt, she decided it was not worth telling him that the woman was Paula.

Such were the events of the night when Paula French disappeared.

6

Love-lorn loon

Rodney and Tiggy had strolled down the garden to the shrubbery at the end, where Kit's tree-house was. It was a morning of radiant sunshine and heat. Rodney wished he could have put her in the car and driven her up into the velvet-grassed, country-fragrant Downs, or to the sea, to the only beach where there was gold sand instead of shingle.

But Doran had gone to Eastgate, and Kit was at play-school in the church hall. Somebody would be bringing him home at lunch-time. They were not free: they never would be free.

Tiggy sat on the swing and propelled herself gently to and fro. She wore a white sleeveless sun-dress, black-dotted. Her creamy shoulders were bare. A wide floppy sunhat shaded her face, giving the effect of a black halo. Even through the scents of the garden her perfume drifted across to Rodney.

'Tell me about Jack Point,' she said on an upward swing, fair eyes throwing enchantment on him beneath the waving brim.

'He was a Fool – in every sense. He sighed for the love of a lady.'

'The all-singing all-dancing girl?'

'Elsie, yes. His travelling partner.'

'Were they living together?'

'Good gracious, no. Victorian audiences couldn't have taken that. He gratuitously hands out the information that her mother, old Bridget Maynard, travels with them, for Elsie is a good girl.'

'Which used to mean a virgin, didn't it?'

'Yes.'

'Then why didn't they get married?'

'Simply because Gilbert knew it would spoil the plot. Point equivocates about it, says time works wonders, all that, but gets very steamed up when they want her to marry Fairfax. He refers to her as "my lovely bride that is to be".' Rodney, lounging on the grass, was picking daisy-heads and throwing them down.

'Don't do that,' Tiggy said. 'It's unkind, not like you. How old was Elsie?'

'Seventeen.'

'And Point?'

Rodney laughed bitterly. 'Fortyish upwards, from the photographs of the mature chaps who've played him. Too old for the job . . .'

Tiggy, not swinging now, regarded him thoughtfully and changed the subject.

'I don't know anything about Gilbert, acksherly.'

'He was a sarcastic, impossible, overbearing man in private life, but uproarious on paper. "*They don't blame you as long as you're funny*," as Point says. It's all there in the *Bab Ballads*, of course. Early nonsense verses, the germs of some of the operas. He had a thing about swopped babies and innocent-looking fiendish girls.'

'Tell me some of your favourites, recite to me,' Tiggy put in quickly. 'Your voice is so beautiful I could go on listening to it, even if it's nonsense.'

'Thanks. All compliments gratefully received in aid of church expenses.' Rodney sat up, his arms round his knees, and assumed a bardic expression.

'*Strike the concertina's melancholy string!*
Blow the spirit-stirring harp like anything!
Let the piano's martial blast
Rouse the Echoes of the Past,
For of Agib, Prince of Tartary, I sing!

'All right so far?'

Tiggy nodded. 'Go on.'

'*Of Agib, who, amid Tartaric scenes,*
Wrote a lot of ballet music in his teens;
His gentle spirit rolls
In the melody of souls –
Which is pretty, but I don't know what it means.'

Tiggy's young laughter, the sunlight on her upturned face, the cleft of her breasts with the single gold chain between them, her parted lips . . .

'Oh, Tiggy,' he said. 'Oh God, I can't keep this to myself any longer. Tiggy . . .'

A face appeared over the fence, pale, anxious, nervous.

'Excuse me,' Euan French said. 'I heard you down here, and I hoped you wouldn't mind my interrupting.'

'Not for a moment,' replied Rodney, who did.

'Is Doran in?'

'No, she's gone to Eastgate.'

'Oh. I wanted to ask her . . . I suppose you don't know? The thing is, Paula's gone. She – wasn't there when I got up this morning, and I wondered if Doran knew anything, if she'd spoken to her yesterday.'

'I'm afraid I've no idea.' With one thought uppermost in his mind, Rodney said, 'You've met Miss Denshaw, Tiggy, have you?'

Euan twitched a smile. 'Doran did make us known to one another, yes. Nice to see you again.' He sighed. 'Oh well then. I suppose I'd better phone people. It's not like her at all. She hasn't phoned or anything. We've had a bit of – well, nastiness, you know – at rehearsals, but not anything to . . . will you ask Doran, when she comes in, please? She seems to get to know things before other people do.'

'Yes, doesn't she? Of course I will. Don't worry, meantime.'

The head disappeared.

'*The Lady Vanishes*,' Rodney said. 'Unregretted, in

this case, I should think. Never mind her, Doran will know.'

'What about Prince – Agib? Do go on.'

'Of Agib, who could readily, at sight
Strum a march upon the loud Theodolite.
He would diligently play
On the Zoetrope all day . . .

'Tiggy, I can't help it. I wasn't going to say it, but I love you so terribly. Go on, tell me I'm a rat, because I love Doran too, she's my wife and of course I love her. But something comes over me . . . I can't explain it. Please forgive me. It had to come out, and though I'm sorry I've said it I'm glad at the same time.'

Tiggy said gravely, 'It's all right, I did know. One can't help knowing, can one? Rodney, I do like you awfully, but Doran's my friend and we couldn't, could we? And acksherly, I don't make a habit of it.' Shaded by the black hat, her cheeks were pink roses.

Rodney made an incoherent sound and picked her up from the seat of the swing. They were tightly locked together, not hearing the gate.

'Hello Daddy, hello Tiggy. Aren't I early? It's vewy vewy hot, isn't it? Can I have an ice cream? Are you hot, too? You look hot.'

'We are,' Tiggy said. 'Let's all go in and have an ice cream, shall we?'

Euan had taken the day off to inquire around the district for his missing wife. His firm were puzzled, suggesting, without quite saying so, that she had gone off in a huff and would be back in time to cook dinner. 'Wouldn't let you down over that.' His boss, Graham, had dined with them and been suitably impressed.

'N-no,' stammered Euan. 'Or even breakfast. She's so proud of her cooking, she'd never leave me to cope on my own.'

'Bet you couldn't, anyway. Well, you can always boil an egg, ha ha.'

Max and Amy were lunching early at the Rose. Max was not pleased at being interrupted in his main meal.

'No, I haven't seen her. No, she said nothing to me. We weren't on close terms.'

'I know,' replied Euan miserably. 'But – you'd been . . .'

'Bloody rude to her. Okay. She asked for it. Why don't you ask that guy – Guy, that's his name, isn't it? He seemed struck enough on her to try to knock one of my teeth out.'

Amy shook her head.

'Well, he loosened it. I could have him up for that. If your Paula's gone off with yon, I wish them both the best.'

When Euan had despondently left, Amy said, 'You shouldn't speak to people like that, Maxie. They're not pros, you should consider their feelings – '

'Bugger their feelings. I like Doran and I like Rodney, he's good on lines and willing to take direction, even if he is a bit . . . dreamy. I don't mind Ruth, she bosses other people but she knows better than to try it on with me. I'm putting up with these other berks on their account. The rest of 'em can all go and . . .'

'Max, people are listening. Don't start again, after last time. It was so awful. And you won't – do anything – at rehearsal?'

Max growled.

Guy Culffe was alone in the photocopying shop in a new development of Barminster, unenthusiastically duplicating council documents. He looked up, startled, at Euan's entrance.

'Hello.' They had not spoken since the fight.

'Have you seen my wife?'

'What?' He stood up, knocking over a pile of papers.

'I asked you if you'd seen Paula. She walked out on me last night. Is she round at your place? I'm asking because I know you fancy her, to say the least of it, after that exhibition the other night.'

Guy turned red, then pale. His hand went to his throat.

'I don't care what you think,' he said. 'She's a wonderful girl, and if anything's happened to her it's because you didn't look after her properly. I only wish she *was* at my place – my sister's place. Shut the door after you.'

Maggie's shop had a Closed sign on the door. Euan drove back to Abbotsbourne, calling at the Firles' home on the way. Annabella, not looking her usual composed self, answered the door.

'No, Paula hasn't been here, and I've no idea where she could be. D'you mind if I don't ask you in? Mummy's not very well.'

When Doran got home from Eastgate two messages awaited her, taken down and faithfully rendered by Tiggy. Euan had telephoned to ask if she was in yet, and if so had she seen or heard anything of Paula.

'He seemed frantic,' Tiggy said. 'He looked dreadful when he spoke to us this morning. How extraordinary of her, walking out on him like that.'

'She's an extraordinary lady. What can he have done, poor man. Unless – '

'What?'

'Nothing.' Paula had been going into the Elvesham woods with Rupert. Could that have started something which ended in a flight from her home?

And Annabella had called, in a shaky, tearful voice, to say that Ruth had wakened that morning feeling unwell, had got worse as the day went on, with a high temperature. The doctor had come very reluctantly, but after examining Ruth he had looked serious and telephoned for an ambulance to take her to Eastgate Hospital.

'Poor Annabella,' Tiggy said, 'she sounded really shaken. Apparently it could be something fairly horrible that Ruth picked up in Sri Lanka when she and Simon were there last month. It's not just flu or anything.'

'Oh dear. So we shan't have a Dame Carruthers tonight.'

'Or an Elsie. Unless she's come back. Your next-door neighbour sounded worried out of his mind.'

Tiggy seemed curiously subdued, Doran thought. Perhaps the heat had affected her. Rodney had gone out with his recorder, leaving a vague message about having to see somebody at Radio Dela.

'Oh well, I shall just have to read for both of them,' Doran said. 'Max is sure to want to carry on with the rehearsal – he's not the sort to care about people being ill or running away . . . Tiggy! I've an idea. They don't really need me for anything tonight – why don't *you* go and read Elsie, if Paula doesn't turn up tonight?'

'Me?' A strange expression, hard to define, flitted across Tiggy's charming features.

'Yes, you'd do it beautifully. Now don't be modest, you know you would. I'll look after Kit. He'll miss you but he'll have to put up with me for a change. I'll get the *Yeomen* book for you.'

'It's all right,' Tiggy said. 'I borrowed Rodney's – just to look at . . .'

The bedtime story was one about monsters, involving a lot of impersonation, roaring and snarling on the reader's part, and some hiding under the bedclothes on the listener's. The monster finally vanquished, not killed but miraculously reformed, Kit reappeared.

'Tiggy's fiercer nor you, Mummy. But I'm not afraid – am I?'

'No, darling. Not a bit.'

'I love Tiggy. I wish she was my sister.' Memories of Helena, of course.

Kit propped himself up on an elbow, clutching the hideous fluorescent rabbit which had been his first favourite toy.

'Daddy loves Tiggy too, Mummy.'

'Yes, we both do.'

'He was kissing her in the garden today, when I come home. Like *vis.*' He shut his eyes tightly and clasped his shoulders. The innocent impression was startlingly vivid. Doran's blood seemed to turn to ice, from feet upwards, though the early evening was oppressively hot. There was a buzzing in her ears: she remembered the sensation of fainting.

'That was nice, darling,' she said, and kissed him quickly, drawing the sheet lightly over him. 'You should be warm enough, but the duvet's there if you want it. Now say your poem until you go to sleep.'

'*Maffew, Mark, LukeanJohn,*
Bless the bed that I lie on . . .'
Kit began obediently.

On the blanket-chest that stood outside Kit's room was a creamware mug, made to celebrate an admiral's victory at sea two hundred years before. It was only in that vulnerable place because it had a hair-line crack and a mended handle, its value lowered. Its inscription ran RODNEY FOR EVER. Doran stared at it, hearing the small voice chanting behind the closed door. What would happen to her, when the numbness wore off? Would there be unimaginable pain?

There was.

In the car on the way to Elvesham Rodney recited the story of Prince Agib, from beginning to end, at the top of his voice and with exaggerated expression.

Tiggy touched his arm, saying, 'There are other drivers, you know. You're getting some funny looks.'

He ignored her.

'They branded me and broke me on a wheel,
And they left me in an hospital to heal;
And upon my solemn word,
I have never never heard
What those Tartars had determined to reveal.'

'Rodney.'

Without looking away from the road, he said, 'Nothing's ever to be said. About this morning. I'm sorry, so sorry, Tiggy.'

Max was delighted by his new Elsie Maynard.

'Can you sing, Gorgeous? You can, just a bit? Then we're made, the show's on. If that bint never comes back it'll be too soon.'

'You've no right to say that,' growled Guy.

'Now you keep off me, or you might get that punch back.'

Rodney intervened. 'The strife is o'er, the battle won. Let's leave it at that, shall we?'

'Okay. Well, we haven't got a full cast, blast it, you realize. No Dame Carruthers, no Shadbolt, no what's-it, First Yeoman, no – where's First Woman Citizen, where's Maggie? Don't tell me, still in the Five Bells. No Doran, so we'll do without props, unless anyone fancies hauling one decrepit spinning wheel and one bloody great kist out here. No? Fat lot of use rehearsing at all. Rodney, you can do without Hugh Ambrose and his Merrie Jestes, use this.' He tossed over a rumpled *Daily Mail*, and transferred himself to the piano. During the entire rehearsal he addressed not one word to Rupert, only monosyllabic barks. The atmosphere between them with Amy as an apprehensive third was thunderous.

The others had heard the beginning of the opera

before, but this was different. Paula's Elsie had been a brittle, confident soubrette. This Elsie, in her first words, conveyed that she was young, very young, accomplished but unsure of herself. She hadn't been travelling with Point very long. She trusted him, but was afraid of the road and its dangers. Her shrinking away from the citizen who roughly grasped at her was real, her shrinking behind her comrade for protection the natural action of a frightened girl.

Max had said that Elsie must be tough and physical. During Point's long jokey speech, cooling the situation, she visibly collected herself, put on her public face and her performer's smile, strengthened her light voice. She read the speeches but had the professional's trick of looking up from the book as she spoke them.

'*Let us give them the singing farce of the Merryman and his Maid – therein is song and dance too.*'

'*I have a song to sing, O.*'

'*Sing me your song, O!*'

The bitter-sweet duet became a tragedy, as these two sang it. The knell of the churchyard bell tolled behind it, the shadow of heartbreak lay over the two who mimed their formal dance. Elsie's hands went out to Point as she finally offered her love: almost apprehensively, seeming hardly daring to believe his luck, he took them in his. Only Tiggy noticed that his were shaking.

The perfect evening was still. In that garden where lavender grew wild, its sharp scent would bring back that rehearsal all their lives, even though its impact was weakened by the stuffy old-vegetable smell of a garden rubbish tip, and the clouds of flies and mosquitoes. Max forgot his annoyance at the missing performers. He had the Elsie he wanted, wherever she'd learned to sing and act like that.

Rupert Wylie forgot the lines he had managed to get by heart. He could hardly take his eyes off this gorgeous little creature. She took his mind off other preoccupations. He was glad that he was playing Colonel Fairfax. Fairfax got the girl, in the end.

At an earlier rehearsal he'd made a blue joke about Elsie's old mother and the electuary Elsie was working to buy her. He was strangely pleased that he'd made it then and not now. He must be going soft, he told himself.

Ralph Chapman, the Lieutenant of the Tower, detached himself from his lines to wonder whether he dare ask Miss Denshaw to sing in St Crispin's choir while she was staying at Abbotsbourne, and what his vicar would say if he did.

Hugo Snaresby wondered whether he dared ask her out to lunch. His wife would never know, if they went to that hotel in Eastgate.

Maggie's eyes were running over with tears. She had taken one more double gin at the Five Bells than she should have done. The performance was moving to one of her emotional nature. And she was so sorry for poor Guy, who was missing Paula.

Poor Guy.

7

Vanished into empty air

Howell sat back and admired a gilt brass carriage clock, then breathed on its glass face before giving it a gentle polish.

'Pretty, isn't it?'

'Very.' Doran was typing at the keyboard of the small, modest computer they had recently allowed themselves.

'French. Margaine. I picked it up very cheap at the sale, Tuesday.'

'Good.'

Howell repressed a sigh. She hadn't even looked up at his prize. Storm clouds rolling up again, by the look of it. Or storm in progress. The clock suddenly broke into frenzied chiming, as though outraged by Howell's tinkering with it. Doran should have laughed and made some comment, but she continued to stare blankly at the screen where line upon line of figures accumulated.

'So what's up?' he asked, stopping the clangour with a touch.

'Our opera production's number is, I should say. Ruth, our contralto – right out of it. She's got some fearful unpronounceable blood disease and they've transferred her to hospital in London. Her husband *was* playing a leading role, but he's half out of his mind with worry. Their Annabella's our scene-painter, and it won't do her a lot of good, either.'

'Bad. Anything else?'

'Oh, just that our leading lady's disappeared. Gone. Vanished. Her husband's half out of his mind, too.

One of the juveniles fancies her madly, so his performance isn't going to improve. And the producer's threatening to walk out when the leading lady comes back.'

'Sounds like Sod's Law rules, then.'

'Yes. It was all in aid of rebuilding Elvesham church tower, but all this has put paid to it – or as good as.'

Howell decided not to comment on whatever else, deeper and more personal, was troubling Doran.

'So this thing can't go on?'

'Well. We've got one or two spare men lying about.' Then, casually, 'Oh, and our London friend who's au-pairing Kit at present's stepped into the female lead. I believe she's very good.'

All Howell's sensitive antennae quivered.

'This would be the Caxton Manor girl, Tiggy Denshaw, of course.' They always avoided saying the name, women did.

'That's right.'

'So if you got a new contralto you might manage?'

Doran shrugged. 'It's Max's affair. I suppose he just might agree to go on, if . . .' Her voice trailed away. Howell sensed her desolation until it became a pain in his own soul. With no wife, no lover, no one particular friend, he cared very much that Doran should not be hurt. There was not much he could do, in this case. Only one thing occurred to him, a very long chance, but worth taking.

'Just got to call someone,' he said, with a wistful glance towards the clock, his morning's work. Doran heard him on the telephone in the shop, next door to the room they used for repairs, accounts and packing. He was speaking Welsh, in which language he sounded quite a different person.

Returning, he said, 'Come on, time we went for a pint.'

'It's not time. It's only half-eleven.' And I daren't drink, she thought, because if I do I shall start talking and it will all come out. Rodney's strangeness in the past few days, the way he looked at Tiggy, her own utter folly in suggesting that Tiggy should stand in for Paula, and Kit's piece of innocent mime, unmistakable in its meaning. To tell Howell would make it all real.

'Time we've walked down the Port Arms, they'll be open. Come on, do you good.'

Outside the Port Arms benches were crowded with drinkers, tourists, locals, boating and fishing folk, gangs of children with Coke tins and crisps. Doran was relieved to see no dealers there. It was their custom to huddle in the fumes of the dark little pub, and in any case opening time was too early for them.

The dark interior was like a cavern, its blackness punctured with red-bulbed brass lamps here and there. Howell led the way through the bar to an alcove, furnished with chairs made from barrels and lighted by a mullioned window.

Somebody was seated there already, a wine glass on the table in front of her. A woman, small and slim, somewhere in her sixties. Her hair, which had been black and determinedly remained so, was twisted up on her head with a jewelled arrow through it: now that was style, Doran thought. The top half of her clothing was black, too, a jersey T-shirt liberally sprinkled with sequins and cabochons forming the outline of a huge butterfly. Her skirt was a blaze of tropical colours, as bright as a Gauguin canvas, and like Gauguin's Tahitian beauties her face was nut-brown, slashed with petunia-pink lipstick.

As soon as Doran met the frank, level stare of the dark eyes, she knew who this was. Howell was saying, 'Mam, this is Doran. Doran, my mam.'

'Pleased to meet you. At last,' said Mrs Evans.

'So am I. I mean, how nice. Somehow I . . .'

If she had gone on with the sentence, Doran would have said that somehow she had imagined Howell's mother as emaciated, prematurely old, showing traces of a hard girlhood and womanhood in a mining valley town, in poorer days than these. There had been a drunken husband, who deserted her, and Howell had on his own admission not been an easy child to bring up. His mother must have been tough: she looked tough. She also looked full of life and light and fun. For a brief moment Doran forgot her own wretchedness.

She turned the sentence into: 'Somehow I never expected Howell to bring you down here.'

'I don't know why not,' returned Mrs Evans, 'seeing I take myself to London and Cornwall and the Lake District – very pretty, that is, though not up to Wales. Coach tours, you know.' Her accent was strongly Welsh, almost stage Welsh, much more so than Howell's, its musical sing-song going on for hypnotic. Her voice too was musical, ranging from deep-toned to middle range.

'Yes,' she went on, 'I thought I'd come and see Hywel's little place now he's got it to himself. Cluttered it is, yes indeed – myself, I would clear a lot of that stuff out, but I can see it would appeal to some kinds of people very much, and Hywel tells me it is worth quite a lot of money.'

Somehow, though the pronunciation was more or less the same, she made it quite clear that her son's name was spelt in the Welsh original form, Hywel.

Howell knew that his mam would go on chattering for as long as it took to calm Doran down and fascinate her, since fascination was Mam's speciality. He had told her on the telephone that his partner was in some sort of emotional trouble, almost certainly connected with her *gwr*, who'd had trouble with his *eglwys* but was still an *offeriad* in a dog collar, and that in his opinion their marriage had reached a point of dullness, Rodney was troubled by the restless forties, and there was a bimbo in the case. There were quite a few Welsh words for such a character, though he knew his mam would very well understand the topical term and all it implied.

Mrs Evans talked, and talked, while Doran listened, as fascinated as Howell had hoped she would be. They drank – the Welshwoman chose a Kir Royale, cassis mixed with an extremely non-vintage champagne, and persuaded Doran to join her. It had a powerfully enlivening effect. The perfume Mrs Evans wore was also powerful, though equally non-vintage. Howell drank beer and listened to his hastily improvised plan working.

At last he said casually, 'Doran's lot up at that church of her husband's are in a terrible mess. They're putting on a Gilbert and Sullivan opera, but one of the opera cast's very ill, and her family's taking it bad, and another of the women's disappeared completely – '

'How old?' interrupted his mother.

Doran thought. 'Early thirties?'

'Pretty, is she?'

'Yes, very, in a . . . yes, she's attractive.'

'Popular? The gentlemen like her?'

'Well. One of them's got a sort of boyish fancy for her and another's taken a fancy that's far from boyish. I wouldn't say the others care much for her.'

'And the women?'

Doran shook her head. Mrs Evans nodded hers.

'Murdered, I daresay you will find.'

'Oh no! Surely nothing so dreadful.'

'They usually are, my dear, when things are like that. Howeffer,' Mrs Evans briskly dismissed the awful possibility, 'if this poor girl is the age you tell me, then I could not replace her. But the sick lady is another kettle of fish, isn't it? As Hywel tells me the opera is *The Yeomen of the Guard* this will be Dame Carruthers, yess?'

Doran looked meaningfully at Howell. So all this

had been discussed already, in that one telephone conversation: it was a plot, against her and for her. She nodded.

'Then I will make so bold as to put myself forward as a replacement. We do a lot of Gilbert and Sullivan, you see, up in the little town in Wales where I live, and I must say, not to seem proud or showing off, I have been much in demand over the years for Dame Carruthers, Katisha, Lady Jane, all those terrible old trouts, you know. I sang in Chapel very powerful when I was a young girl, indeed I thought I would become an opera singer but there was no money. So you see – ?'

'Yes, I see,' Doran said. 'Thank you very, very much. Have another drink.'

Howell, who had not contributed a word to this, brought more drinks from the bar, and carried his own off in the direction of a friend he claimed to have seen. Doran, into her second Kir, suddenly felt an almost overpowering urge to pour out her feelings to Mrs Evans. She'd been through a lot of life and trouble, she'd know how it would be to realize that one's adored husband for four years, and adored lover before that, had fallen for somebody else. She would know how to cope – whether to speak to either of them, what attitude of mind to take, how best to disguise her jealous misery with the girl actually under her own roof.

The dark eyes flashed up at her. They said to her, without words: Keep your own counsel. If there was a Welsh proverb equivalent to 'Patience, and shuffle the cards', she was being advised to act on it.

'Mrs Evans . . .' she began, but was interrupted.

'My name is Gwenllian. Please use it.'

It appeared that Gwenllian was quite prepared to give a lot of time to rehearsals. There was almost nothing to do in Eastgate of an evening, she said, and Hywel would be glad to have her out from under his feet. She had a little hire-car, to make her independent of him. Howell seemed pleased by the arrangement. It meant that somebody he could trust absolutely was going to be in a position to keep an eye on Doran in what he guessed to be a dodgy situation.

Max, after a suspicious private audition, declared himself astonished and delighted by the new Dame Carruthers.

'If the Tower of London had a singing voice it would be like hers. By God, these Welsh can sing! All right, I'll stay on. But one more drop-out and you've lost me.'

As Ruth was now in intensive care, Simon felt that he must stay in London near her. That removed Shadbolt. The gently persuasive arguments of Ralph Chapman's one-time vicar, Rodney, talked him into taking on the part, though his substitute as Lieutenant of the Tower, a colourless stick of a man called Alex Warner, who worked in the Abbotsbourne bank, confessed to being unable to sing a note. His lyrics were hastily removed and turned into speech, which made complete havoc of the famous Act One ending.

But somehow it would work.

Doran steeled herself into attending rehearsal, to introduce Gwenllian. Kit was being nannied by Vi Small. Gwenllian needed no nannying. She turned the full heat of her electric personality on the rest of the cast, and met no resistance. What a mercy, Doran thought, that Paula wasn't there.

Having stormed through her first short scene Gwenllian sat back and observed. Doran, taut with repressed anxiety, trying not to look at Rodney and Tiggy. Rodney, apparently cool, self-possessed, wearing his public face and giving nothing away. Tiggy, pretty thing, in love and showing it, to a sharp pair of Welsh eyes.

Rupert Wylie, drooling over Tiggy. A lecher, a fifth-rate Giovanni. Euan French, present because there was nothing he could do at home but wait for the return of his wife: a poor, unmanned thing, a widower already in his own mind. Guy Culffe – now there was a dangerous one, a youth sick in mind. Maggie, hiding something – what? – behind dark glasses. Amy, the Seer. And beside her, on the grass, the cheap pink teddy bear she called her Teddy-charm.

Gwenllian had met Teddy before rehearsal. Amy, ever anxious to be nice to newcomers, came up and introduced them.

'It's like having a dog when you're out for a walk, people come and speak to you. He's lovely, isn't he, my Teddy-charm?'

Gwenllian had a good line in mendacity.

'Quite amazing, he is.' Privately she wouldn't have permitted such an object within streets of her grandchild, if she had been lucky enough to have one. 'Bit on the large side for a charm, though?'

'Ah. That's his little secret. He's magic, you see, he can take spells off and lift curses.' Truly a remarkable gift, thought Gwenllian, considering that he had been mass-produced in Taiwan within the fairly recent past. 'I put him on to that spinning wheel, the one Phoebe uses in Act One. Do you know, when I first went near that thing I felt the most fearful blast of evil from it. It's old, of course – Doran found it somewhere – who knows what awful tragedies it may have seen? Thank God they're keeping the props inside in case we have a storm overnight. But I thought it was so clever of Max to hire a piano on castors, so it can live in its little stable.' She nodded towards the shed which had once housed Primary Scholastic bicycles, and was now occupied by rusting garden tools and rubbish. 'Don't you think my Max accompanies brilliantly? Oh, I shouldn't say that, I know.' But she looked pleased that she had. Gwenllian swiftly worked out the length of their marriage – five years, perhaps less – the near-certainty that Amy was Max's second wife, and the probability that there was a touch of Latin or Celt in this refreshingly emotional Englishwoman. Even if she did believe in unconvincing magic charms.

The closing moments of Act One were drawing near. The cheated Point heard that his Elsie's bridegroom had escaped from his prison cell, and reacted with bitter sarcasm.

'*Oh, woe is* you? *Your anguish sink.*
Oh, woe is me, *I rather think!*
Yes, woe is me, *I rather think!*'

There would have been a fine ensemble to end the act if Alex Warner had been able to sing. As it was, he chanted his lines against the dramatic chorus music.

'*All frenzied with despair we rave,*
The grave is cheated of its due . . .'

Tiggy moaned, to indicate the collapse of Elsie in Fairfax's arms. Rupert smirked. Fairfax was not going to neglect the opportunity. It would be nice to have her utterly at his mercy, on stage, where she couldn't run away.

Jack Turner, the Headsman, had objected to rehearsing when he was not needed for singing, but Max had overruled him. He stood impassively, arms folded on the crook of his umbrella. Max, eyeing him, decided that by the weekend they would be rehearsing with props, and be damned to all this open-air stuff. He crashed out the final, fateful chords, and everyone let out pent-up breath and started chattering.

'Extraordinary woman,' said Rodney, at home.

'Very.' Doran's voice was toneless. Rodney glanced sharply at her. Tiggy had gone to bed, tired. Vi had gone home, after reporting that Kit seemed wrong side out tonight.

'Not been really himself since Miss Denshaw came. She spoils him, if you ask me.'

'Yes, I expect she does,' Doran agreed. She's spoiled everything. Why did I ever ask her to stay? I might have known. Rodney's forty-three, just the age to fall. It's not her fault, and she *is* very attractive, I saw the men eyeing her . . . For an alarmed moment she thought she was speaking aloud. But Vi was saying to Rodney that the heat was unnatural in her opinion, and a thunderstorm would do a world of good.

'Sorry to make you babysit every evening, Vi,' Rodney said, 'but at least you can be in the garden and still hear Kit from upstairs.'

'Oh, I don't bother, not with them mosquitoes thinking it's Christmas and I'm their dinner. And anyway, like I told you, my friend Hayley's going to take turns with me. Trust Hayley with anything, you could, she's as steady as a rock.'

And as plain as a pikestaff, reflected Doran with satisfaction. Her thoughts rambled darkly on behind Vi's departure. I'd have trusted Tiggy with anything, too. And she's been so kind to me, putting me up in London, and giving Kit all those presents, and asking us to go and stay at Brighton at her grandmother's, when Nan was away in Greece later in the year. Oh, Tiggy! how could you?

If it's true.

Rodney was back on the topic of Gwenllian. 'Quite amazing. I'd have expected Howell's mother to be a grim lady like something out of *Under Milk Wood* – Mrs Organ Morgan, do I mean? No teeth and a voice like a power drill.'

'She's seen a lot of trouble. It wouldn't be surprising if she were like that. But she's got astonishing resilience. Howell says she lives it up as much as anyone can within the limits of a Welsh village – she's the life and soul of a local eatery. The owner's her boyfriend, in fact. He gives her things all the time, clothes, house gadgets, costume jewellery . . .'

'But not a wedding ring.'

'No. Apparently they both have too much sense for that.'

Rodney automatically became Jack Point. '*Though I'm a fool, there's a limit to my folly.*' Then was sorry he'd chosen that line.

A silence followed. Rodney's thoughts were as busy as Doran's. Her manner was odd tonight. But she couldn't know. And there was nothing to know, and never would be. It was all a romantic fantasy and he intended to keep it that way.

'Speaking of matrimony,' he said, 'no news about the missing Paula?'

'Nothing. Euan went home early in case there was a phone call, but obviously there wasn't. By the way, Gwenllian said an odd thing to me, about Paula . . .'

Upstairs a faint wailing began.

'I'll go and see what he wants,' Rodney said.

Doran listened to his swift footsteps on the stairs. She was ashamed to wonder if they would pause at Tiggy's bedroom door on the way from the nursery. She looked at the clock, and began to count the minutes until he came down again. But that was ridiculous. *Alas, I waver to and fro: Dark danger hangs upon the deed . . . His pains were o'er and he sighed no more, For he lived in the love of a lady . . .*

Sam Eastry, Detective-Inspector, just about to go home after a day of slogging at office work in a temperature well up in the eighties, was recalled to his desk by the telephone. He said a word which seldom passed his lips.

The caller was Glen Lidell, his successor as Abbotsbourne's community policeman. A diligent young man, still enthusiastic about his work (and well he might be, thought Sam) he was reporting something his superior might like to know about the missing Abbotsbourne woman.

'What missing Abbotsbourne woman? Nobody's told me about one.'

Glen explained about the disappearance of Paula French. He was surprised that Doran hadn't been on to her old friend Sam about it.

So was Sam. He missed Doran, as he missed so much about his old home. He had been her confidant in the days when she needed one, before her marriage, her counsellor, someone who took the place of her long-dead father. Now he had a most precious little daughter of his own, but he still missed Doran.

'She must have other things on her mind, Glen, or she'd have given me a bell. Has this business something to do with her?'

Glen said that it had – she even lived next door to the vanished Mrs French. 'But what I wanted to tell you is that Mrs French was seen, the night she left home, up at Elvesham, near the place where they were rehearsing. It's an absolutely kosher sighting, because the person who saw her was my Kate.'

Kate, Glen's wife, was appropriately enough Abbotsbourne's community nurse, a brisk young woman who was a valued conveyor of news to the villagers, happy to chat about anything and anyone provided that no medical ethics were involved. Busy as her life and Glen's were, it had only been that morning when she got round to telling him about her glimpse of Mrs French.

'Kate had been on a maternity case, and the baby didn't arrive until going on for midnight. She was driving through Elvesham when she saw Mrs French, running hell for leather towards the Old Primary School. Kate thought it was funny, because she's such a smart lady usually, and there she was looking half crazy, with her hair all over the place – Kate particularly noticed her hair.'

'I see. What was she wearing?'

'A light coat of some sort – Kate couldn't see what else.'

Sam took more details. If an investigation arose, they might well be needed. No parked car visible, nobody else about. Kate had thought of stopping and offering a lift, but it was pretty obvious that Mrs French must have got there by car, and would presumably be going home in it. No, Kate hadn't looked for Mrs French's car, and probably wouldn't have recognized it if she had. She was tired and anxious to get home to bed. She didn't think any more about the incident until she heard from a patient next day about Mrs French's disappearance.

'That's all there is. Thought you might like to know. Funny that you hadn't heard – funny that *I* hadn't, come to that. Not that I'd have taken it too seriously, her going missing. Women do strange things, especially after a few words. And Mrs F. had a bit of a temper, according to one or two reports.'

Sam thanked him and hung up. Doran would have told him all this, once, would have made it her business to find out, she with her eager curiosity, and to pass on the information. It wasn't like her.

As he travelled home to his longed-for garden, it was not Paula French he worried about, but Doran.

The oppressive heat built itself up to a prelude to storm. At Bell House open doors and windows let in air that was like the perimeter of a blast furnace. The drawing room door stood open, because Rodney and Tiggy were rehearsing in there at the piano, and neither was going to risk their being alone together, even though Doran went to Eastgate every day and Kit went to the church play-school Mrs Dutton nobly kept open and ran personally.

By unspoken agreement, they avoided touching. The atmosphere was charged with an electricity which owed nothing to the weather. Tiggy was glad to escape and do the shopping, a relief from the sight of Rodney's taut face. She was buying in the greengrocer's when an arm came round her waist from behind.

'Morning, Beauty. Care for a lift from the Beast?'

'Oh, Rupert. No, I wouldn't, thanks.'

'With all that shopping? Two tons of new potatoes included? Come on, it's all free.'

'Too free, if you ask me. Anyway, I'm used to carrying things, and it's good for the figure.'

He surveyed the figure. 'Thirty-five, six – twenty-four – thirty-six? That right?'

'No, several inches out, not that it's anything to do with you.' She was filling a plastic bag with carrots from the self-service counter.

'Oh, but it is! I'm your Colonel Fairfax, remember? *Mistress Elsie, there is one here who, as thou knowest, loves thee right well.*'

'Yes, *and a glance of despair is no guide – it may have it's ridiculous side, It may draw you a tear Or a box on the ear – You can never be sure till you've tried.*'

'I *am* trying.'

'Looks like a sickly leer from where I'm standing. And people are listening to us. Rupert, do be a nice man and leave me alone. You don't know me, I've dodged more wandering hands than any au pair from Grosvenor Square to Hyde Park Gate. It's no use, now sod off.' The last two words were spoken softly but firmly, for Rupert's ears only, since other customers' ears were out on stalks like snails' eyes. He shrugged, picked up a plum, bit it, and walked out without paying.

So, he reflected moodily, eyeing the property ads in

his own shop window, that would have to be that. His desirable property was no longer Under Offer. He would have another go at Doran that night. She ought to be a pushover, low as she was over Rodney being out of his mind over Tiggy (so much for parsons). He would try the old trick after rehearsal that night. It had worked with Doran once. And she wasn't a bad lay.

Doran drove home faster than she liked to drive. The tourist season was at its height and she and Howell were both needed at the shop to deal with droppers-in and lingerers, sometimes light-fingered. The car had been standing in the sun and was almost unbearably hot. Sweat ran into her eyes from her dankly dripping curls. She wore driving gloves because her hands and the wheel were equally slippery. The sky was a threatening grey purple, hanging low over the approaching Downs. Dark danger again. What were they doing now, at home? This sort of heat was said to increase the passions. To distract her thoughts, she began to sing.

'*Is life a thorn? then count it not a whit,*
Nay, count it not a whit, man is well done with it . . .'

Rodney met her in the hall. 'You're late,' he greeted her.

Oh, you did notice, then. Thanks. 'Yes. We were busy and the roads are packed.'

'Max rang. He says we'll have to rehearse in the hall tonight.'

'I'd worked that out – there are great spots of rain coming down now. Oh, well – I'm the SM, I'd better go and unlock and set the stage now, before I get changed. Where's the key?'

'What key?'

'Oh, Rodney. The key of the Old Primary School. We rehearse there, remember? It's on that wire ring with all the other keys, for Shadbolt to carry.'

Rodney looked completely blank. Then comprehension dawned. 'Oh, I was supposed to lock up, last time we rehearsed in there. Wasn't I?'

'Yes. And I was supposed to remind you, and I didn't. Was the school open while we were rehearsing outside, then?' She tried to remember whether anyone had gone in and out. Paula had said something about fetching her costume hat, but hadn't. The piano: had they taken that in? No, the men had wheeled it into a shed in the school garden. Then she remembered.

'We put the chairs away, as we'd done the two previous nights. So it must have been open. Then who locked it, if it *is* locked – which I hope it is, because the props and things aren't insured yet. Oh Heavens, I should have done that. Suppose something's been nicked?'

Tiggy had appeared from the kitchen, pale and beautiful as only she could be with the barometric pressure at its height. She and Rodney did not exchange looks, and then, determinedly, did. By this time Doran's mind was on the worry of the possibly unlocked door, and her reactions to atmosphere slower than usual.

'Someone *must* have collected the key, on a great ring like a bicycle wheel,' she said. 'I must rush up there and make sure things are all right.'

'But how will you get in, if the door's locked?' Tiggy asked reasonably.

Doran tugged at her hair. 'Oh, good question – how on earth . . . ? I know. There's a little door round the back, near the loos, with one of those catches you can open with a credit card. And yes, I do know how to, because we had a small break-in at the shop and the police showed me. Right. Follow me as soon as you can, both of you.'

They heard her car start up and roar off.

'Well, I must get back to Kit,' Tiggy said. Now was

the time to be thoroughly matter of fact. 'As soon as Vi arrives we can go.'

Rodney longed to say something, he hardly knew what, about themselves. Instead he said, 'She's never late. I must go and get the deckchairs in . . .'

8

Death in most appalling shape

The raindrops pattered thickly on the bonnet of the car as Doran drove along the twisting upward road to Elvesham. The pattering became a thudding as they turned to hail, a deafening fusillade. The windscreen wipers swept in busy arcs and the sky grew dark as night. Doran prayed that any cars coming the opposite way would have their lights on.

Thunder growled. After a few seconds a flash of lightning ripped the darkness. Not too far away, that. She was glad to see the first cottages of Elvesham appear on each side of the gleaming, slippery road ahead, then the turn that would take her to the Old Primary School.

Elvesham was deserted, small wonder, except for a boy running with a newspaper over his head. The lightning flashes came faster, great jagged forks. Doran was not afraid of storms – they could be exciting and dramatic, especially seen from indoors, but she was less than thrilled by the prospect of being out in one like this.

The little war memorial appeared. That meant she was almost at the school. She parked, thankfully, next to what had been the playground wall and pulled over her head an old coat she kept in the back seat. As she turned from locking the car a particularly brilliant dazzle of lightning showed her a figure dodging out from behind the memorial. It was a man, and she recognized his face – Ken Wedderbell, the odd dealer from whom she had rented out some props. There was no mistaking him, although his strange face now seemed in some way distorted.

For an instant they confronted each other, then he turned and vanished.

What had he been doing there? The little memorial was hardly a shelter, just a stone Celtic cross about ten feet high, on a plinth. And why was he at Elvesham? There had been no mention of it when she visited him with Peg. The tall bent figure, livid-faced, had looked like something out of a Hammer horror film, curious and disturbing.

But the urgent thing was to get round the building and through the small door at the back (the main door had been locked, after all). Wet hands and a wet credit card made the job of breaking in more difficult than it had seemed when demonstrated by the police, but after a struggle the lock yielded.

It was a relief to be indoors, dripping as she was. She groped for the light switches and found the one for the main hall. It was a cheerless sight, a few chairs left over from those taken up to the stage, the walls hung with some large, heavily foxed prints of classical architecture and a number of group photographs. Ex-pupils and their teachers, presumably, from the early days of the school up to the immediate postwar years. The faces looked at her, solemn and unreal. How old were they now, those children? Even supposing they were all still alive, which seemed unlikely. Doran shivered. She was glad of the air purifiers she had scattered about the hall.

The lighting switches for the stage were numerous and complicated. Doran settled for one that would give her enough light to move the objects huddled in the opposite–prompt corner.

But what a fool she'd been, to come here alone in such a hurry – even though she'd had good reason for haste.

'I'm never going to be able to shift this lot myself,' she said aloud, partly in order to hear a human voice and partly from an uneasy sensation that some other presence was there with her, unseen. Wedderbell, following her in? Or someone else?

If the atmosphere had been bad in the hall it was far worse up here on the stage, not so much stuffy as mephitic. Obviously, nobody had thought to leave any windows open during the garden rehearsals, and some sort of perfume had gone stale on the air. Doran remembered Gwenllian's – but she had never rehearsed indoors. On the canvas slung behind the stage, with a ladder up in front of it, Annabella's unfinished outline of the Tower loomed down. All very Gothick and rather nasty. But the props were all there, safe.

'Oh, well,' said Doran loudly to the invisible hearer, 'better make a start.' Rodney wouldn't want the *Booke of Jestes* visible, he'd have to carry it on from the dressing room. She took it down to where the costumes hung on dress-rails and put it on the prop-table.

The block. That was only cardboard weighted with sand. She put it beside the book. In fact, only Elsie's spinning wheel was needed on stage at first, then Elsie was supposed to carry it off. Rather her than me, thought Doran, struggling with its awkward shape. But, used as she was to moving furniture, she managed to get it to the square she had marked for it in chalk. There seemed nothing sinister about it to her, but then she wasn't the super-sensitive Amy. In any case, Amy had probably been unconsciously influenced by the atmosphere.

Or stench, one might say. Oh God, ought I to ask the Health people to step along and check for rats, or sewage, or something? But there isn't time, if they needed to take the boards up . . .

The chest. That would have to be off-centre left, so that it wouldn't get in the way of the crowd movement.

Yes, there was the chalk mark. But how to get it there, with her own hands? It was far too heavy. She stood back and surveyed it by the light that barely showed its grotesque detail.

What a beast, when she could have picked a perfectly decent plain one and mocked it up with some sort of drapery. The carved monsters looked grimmer than they had in Wedderbell's basement. The wolves' snarls were fiercer, the gargoyles leered diabolically, the monks' demeanour suggested that the Dissolution of the Monasteries had come not a moment too soon.

And a cloud of flies had scattered at her touch.

A very unpleasant cold sensation crept through Doran, in spite of the heat.

She made herself, with considerable effort, approach the chest again and raise the heavy lid with both hands. Instantly the stench rushed up at her, and there was no mistaking it this time.

Sacks. A bundle of what looked like garden sacks. More flies, crawling about on them, too languid to escape. And, between the sacks, scarlet fabric.

Unthinkable to touch the sacking with her hands. Doran picked up a paintbrush from a jar left by Annabella, and with the handle gingerly stirred it apart.

The scream she gave tore the silence as the lightning had torn the skies. The chest was a coffin, and the half-wrapped corpse it held could only have been that of one person, though the face was unrecognizable. A great gash of blackened blood was between it and the body, which was recognizable enough. Paula French had gone to her awful death wearing the Elsie Maynard costume of scarlet taffeta. But it was tarnished now by the great effusion of blood which had streamed over it. The perfume *Je Rêve* mixed horribly with other odours. A light coat was rolled up beside the corpse, and the little red hat, stained almost out of recognition, lay at its feet, beside a pale – once pale – handbag.

Doran could never remember what she did, except that she found herself back at the small open door, still shrieking, and reeled out into the yard at the back, where she was extremely sick.

She came back to awareness of what was happening. Somebody was holding her head in a very professional manner, and a female voice was saying, 'There now. Better? Whateffer is the matter?'

'Gwenllian,' said Doran faintly. 'Gwenllian.'

People were arriving. Sitting on a low wall with her head in her hands, Doran was aware of voices, more and more of them, Max's shout, Amy's excited questions, an agonized cry from a man who might be Euan or Guy, and Gwenllian's sing-song dominating the lot. It was difficult to think clearly, though she tried. The storm had passed, with just a few sullen drops still falling, and there was a steady downpour from the gutters.

Suddenly Gwenllian was beside her again.

'Drink this. I sent Maggie down to the pub for it. Do you good.'

It was brandy, immediately effective. At last she was able to speak.

'What's happening?'

'Well, they're all turning up. Max phoned 'em all and said to come when the storm was over. I've broken the news, as you might say, and called the police from the box outside.'

'You're being marvellous.'

'Oh, it's nothing,' said Howell's mother. 'I like organizing people, you know, and I seen murder before.'

'So have I, as it happens, but not like this one.'

'No, nasty, very. You come inside, now, there's a nice young policeman arrived, and we're all going to talk this over quietly. I've covered . . . there's nothing to see now, and no one has. You hold on to me, *merch*.'

How curious. Howell called her 'daughter' in his own language, too. Her cold hand grasped firmly in a small warm one, Doran meekly followed Gwenllian into the school. Glen Lidell, looking serious and flustered, was going from one person to another with his notebook, and occasionally using his walkie-talkie. He looked up from it and told them all, 'CID's on their way from Barminster. Nobody's to leave, please.'

'Does he know who it is?' Doran whispered.

'Yes, I told him it was Mrs French – it was, wasn't it? – and he's passed that on.' She forebore to add that Glen had taken a quick look at the contents of the chest and gone very quickly outside for a minute. Road accidents so far had been almost his only experience of violent death.

Max, grim-faced, had his arm tightly round Amy. Maggie was holding Guy against her as though she were a large hen and he her chicken. His face was the colour of paper. Euan was sitting in a corner by himself, his head in his hands. Rupert, looking concerned, was walking up and down restlessly. Jack Turner was missing, but then he always turned up late because he disliked standing around, otherwise the entire cast was present.

Except Jack Point and Elsie.

Vi had not turned up.

Such a little time had passed, and yet their lives were changed. They had not noticed the storm, in Tiggy's bed in the old room where Helena had once slept. They had not heard Kit calling for them in the kitchen, frightened by the lightning into taking refuge in a cupboard with the cat. The deckchairs remained out in the rain, soaked.

Tiggy emerged from the bathroom, fastening the tiny

gilt buttons of her frock. Her face was pale and solemn. Rodney stared at her as though she were a complete stranger. And so she was, in those particular circumstances. A pretty girl of great sweetness of character, who had reminded him strongly of Doran as she had been when he first knew her, and he had been charmed into a middle-aged infatuation which had led him to betray Doran.

And now he felt nothing, no sense of exultant conquest. Only a bitter regret for his behaviour, remorse for Doran and for Tiggy. The Bard had got it right with *The expense of spirit in a waste of shame Is lust in action.*

Tiggy read his look. She came to sit beside him on the bed.

'It's all right, Rodney. Stop worrying. I'm a bit rocked, too. It had to happen, to me as well as you. Neither of us meant it to, but it did. Perhaps it was the storm.'

'But you . . .'

'I'm okay. In my sort of work one has to be prepared for anything. And acksherly I liked it, I'm so glad it was you. I'll always remember.' Her breathing was slowing down, her colour coming back. 'But the person that matters is Doran. Rod, I know exactly how you feel, you think you ought to go to the Archbishop or somebody and ask him to excommunicate you, and then you'd go and tell Doran and beg her to forgive you. I've been thinking about this. Just in these few minutes.'

'Yes.'

'Well, you mustn't. It would be the cruellest thing you could do, and I mean that. I think she guesses we've had a bit of a thing going, but we must never let her know this happened. Nobody else knows, nobody's going to tell her. Just make some sort of joke of it, when you've pulled yourself together – about you falling for me, I mean. If you feel you must talk about it, get hold of a parson friend, *not* Mr Dutton, preferably a Catholic priest, they've heard it all, and tell him. That way you'll get it out of your system and feel a lot better. Okay?'

'You're a very wise young woman,' Rodney said with awe.

'I was very well brought up. Lord, look at the time! Vi *must* be here in a minute and goodness knows where Kit is . . .' She heard herself sounding affected. She had known the time, every second of it.

Rodney brightened a little. *'Temptation, oh temptation,'* he said.

Tiggy nodded. 'Exactly. Just like the Trio in Act One. We fell head over heels into it, and now we're out again. Simple.'

He would never know how deeply she had fallen into love with him. Or how hard it had been to have to pretend. That too was a confession not to be made, ever.

To Doran's intense relief Sam was in charge. He had been in Barminster when the call went out, near enough to be at Elvesham before the unhappy people in the school had waited twenty minutes. A tough-looking young plain-clothes man, Sergeant Dews, was with him. Sam caught Doran's eye and gave her a smile, which she badly needed. She was missing Rodney, wondering desperately where he was.

The three policemen went up to the stage and dragged the coffer out of sight, masking it with the spinning wheel draped in a cloak. Everyone tried not to watch their half-seen operations, but it was impossible to look in any other direction. A photographer joined them and a man Doran knew to be a police doctor. It was, she thought, like some dreadful half-glimpsed shadow play.

Sam came down to them, and now he was not smiling.

'I'm afraid I shall have to ask you all to move. We need a bit more space.' At Gwenllian's suggestion they filed into the dressing room used by the women of the cast. The chairs were carried through, the dress-rails moved back against the walls, and Gwenllian made everybody a cup of tea from the equipment kept by the old stone sink. What should we have done without her? Doran wondered.

After what seemed like hours but were actually minutes, filled with sounds and voices from the hall, Sam rejoined them. He sat down, no longer Doran's familiar Sam but an impersonal, official policeman.

'I have something very unpleasant to tell you, ladies and gentlemen. I find it hard to put it in an acceptable way. But we have to face facts.' He paused.

Rupert muttered under his breath, 'Get on with it.'

'The body of Mrs Paula French has been found in a carved chest which was to be used as a stage property, I believe. She has been murdered. By decapitation. Her head has been severed from her body by a sharp cutting instrument, probably the chopper we found nearby with a quantity of pikes.'

After the first appalled taking-in of the news the listeners reacted in wordless cries, a scream from Amy, a shouted 'No!' from Maggie. Euan went out into the yard. Guy began to scream, short sharp screams like someone enduring an old-style dentist's drill. The other men's faces were greenish.

But Jack Turner the butcher slipped sideways off his chair and fell heavily to the ground in a dead faint.

'I killed her,' he gasped after they brought him round.

'Make sense, man,' Max said. 'You can't have done.'

'I tell you I did.'

Sergeant Dews unobtrusively switched on his recorder.

Sam said, 'I think you'd better tell us about it, Mr Turner. You mean you deliberately killed Mrs French?'

'No, no, nothing of the sort.' Beads of sweat were standing out on the butcher's pale face. 'It's my chopper, you see, I lent it to 'em.'

'Yes. But that doesn't make you – '

'Let me finish. When I got it here I thought it'd look pretty shabby on the stage, make me look a right poor hand as a butcher. I've got to stand up there, you know, waving this chopper, waiting for him' – he pointed at Rupert – 'to be brought to t'block. So I wanted the bloody thing to look as if I'd got it fit for the job, and I took it home again and sharpened it.'

Sam overlooked the unfortunately apt adjective. 'That was a dangerous thing to do, Mr Turner.'

'I know that now, don't I? Well, when I got it back here I put it out in the shed, that lean-to where there's some rakes and shovels and clutter. I don't know how it got itself in here.'

The situation in the dressing room was rapidly getting out of hand. It was obvious to Sam that some of the company were unfit for present questioning. Guy seemed to be in hysterics, Amy was begging Max to take her home, Euan was in the garden, pacing about, not responding to requests to come in. Rupert was blustering about his complete non-involvement in the whole thing, and using language unsuitable to a mixed gathering. Sam came over to Doran, who, with Gwenllian, was sitting quietly, half shadowed by the hanging costumes, waiting for the awfulness to stop. Nothing, however unendurable it seemed, went on for ever.

'You two ladies are being very good about this. You both saw the body, I understand.'

Doran nodded.

Sam's heart bled for Doran. He, of those who were there, was most aware of her vulnerability. He sensed that what troubled her as well as her shocking discovery of Paula was the absence of Rodney from the scene.

'I think you ought to go home,' he said. 'Would you – would you very kindly go with Doran, Mrs Evans?'

'Never you doubt that. I've got my little car outside.'

'Good. Can we have a word first? Just Mrs Chelmarsh.'

Gwenllian went out, with the smallest of flounces. Doran paused beside Sam.

Sam lowered his voice to ask Doran, 'Can you be here at nine forty-five tomorrow? I'd be grateful for an early word. Sorry to ask you.'

'No bother.'

'I'm going to take the chance of letting the others go. There's no obvious suspect – this was probably an unpremeditated crime by an outsider. I'm going to use this place as a Murder Incident Room and we'll ask the questions tomorrow.'

He turned to inform the company of this. Rupert stamped out before he had finished speaking. Sergeant Dews had brought Euan in from the garden, and was half holding him upright. Doran had never seen a more ravaged face, made old in minutes by shock, the face of a tortured being in Dante's *Inferno*.

'All right, everybody,' Sam told them. 'Go home now. I'll expect you all here at ten o'clock tomorrow morning, so that we can find out what everybody knows about this wretched business. The body's been removed, photographs taken, and nobody is to approach or touch the stage. Thank you.'

Doran lingered as the others left, Guy already quieter after the sedative administered by the police doctor, Euan submitting to being driven home by a sergeant, Max very subdued, his arm round Amy's shoulders.

'I reckon that's my production down the drain. Good riddance,' Doran heard him say.

Amy leaned heavily on his arm. 'I knew that spinning wheel had a curse on it,' she murmured.

'It wasn't the spinning wheel,' Doran informed nobody in particular. 'It was the coffer. Or coffin.' She began to laugh, stopping abruptly as Rodney appeared in the doorway.

'Oh, Doran, my darling.' Then she was in his arms, held fast and safe. Tiggy was not with him.

Later he explained, mentally thanking God that the explanation was true.

'We waited for Vi to turn up and look after Kit. It got to seven o'clock and I didn't know what to do. I was just going round to ask Celia Dutton if she'd take over when Hayley Whatshername, you know, arrived and said Vi had slipped on her garden path and given her knee a nasty wrench, so Hayley had volunteered instead. None of them have telephones, of course.'

'Then where's Tiggy?'

'One of the police team rang. Sam told him to, apparently. When we knew what had happened Tiggy said she'd only be in the way. So I came to get you.'

What Tiggy had said was, 'Right. There's nothing I can do, and it's you she'll want to see, so go and be very, very kind to her and *don't let her guess*. If you do, I'll add you to the quota of murderees. You see if I don't. Remember our duet? *It is sung with a sigh and a tear in the eye, For it tells of a righted wrong, O?* I'm going to prepare a really terrific dinner with a half of champagne to start, and never mind if it's in bad taste, what matters is Doran.'

Because of certain hints dropped in her ear by the police, the meal Tiggy prepared was not only vegetarian but artistically planned as a symphony in pastel shades.

9

Who hath contrived this deed to do?

The Old Primary School was looking its best, for what that was worth, on the bright clear morning following the storm. But Doran was reluctant to enter it with the happenings of that night playing over and over in her mind, like memories of a horrible film one had been forced to see. The young policeman on guard at the door smiled pleasantly on her, enjoying the sunshine. He failed to smile on yet another hopeful reporter.

Already police rule had taken over. The body of the hall contained only chairs, tidily arranged. The stage, Doran was glad to see, had been cleared but for the Tower canvas. Nastily apt, Dame Carruthers's song. *Insensible, I trow, as a sentinel should be, Though a queen to save her head should come a-suing . . .*

Yet another constable led her to the right-hand dressing room. That, too, had been transformed. The dress-rails had been pushed alongside the walls, the central space was now occupied by a folding table, several chairs, and the usual appurtenances of a travelling police station.

Sam sat by the table. Doran thought fleetingly how much he had changed since his transfer to Eastgate – he looked years older, heavier and more careworn. But the old Sam smiled as he greeted her and beckoned his sergeant to bring her a chair.

'Nobody else rolled up yet?' she asked.

'No. They're not usually too eager, unless they're hungry for publicity. I'll sort them out separately when they do. This is Sergeant Dews, by the way. But I wanted to talk to you first, as you were the finder of the body.'

'Deceased. That's the usual term in evidence, isn't it, without even the definite article?'

Sam shook his head in reproof. He knew Doran's state of mind when she chattered like this.

'Don't worry, I'm not going to ask you any gruesome questions. It's just very helpful to me to have someone personally known to me involved with a case like this, where the other people are largely new country. The Firles I know, of course – tragic about that, I hear that Mrs Firle's no better, still in intensive care. Bright girl, that Annabella of theirs – I'd like my Jennifer to turn out like that. Now, first let's go over your discovery.' He nodded at the impassive-faced sergeant, who switched on his inconspicuous recorder and posed a pen over his notebook.

They went over Doran's arrival the previous evening, and what had followed it, Sam asking occasional questions and tactfully sliding over the moment when she had opened the coffer.

'Seems a silly question, Doran – but was this a complete shock to you? Apart from the unpleasantness of it, I mean?'

Doran thought. 'Well. I'd never thought of Paula French turning up dead, especially in that way. And yet . . . somebody did say to me, after she went missing, that they guessed she'd been murdered.'

'Oh? Someone who knew her well?'

'They didn't know each other at all. It was Howell's mother – you met her last night.'

'Ah. The little Welsh parakeet. Startling lady. Now has she said since the discovery that she knew or guessed at murder beforehand, or . . . scrub that, Dews. Sorry, Doran, I'd no right to ask you that. I'll be questioning her myself in Eastgate.'

'I'll tell you, anyway – she never mentioned it, and I'd completely forgotten it until this minute.'

'Ah. Was she popular, Mrs French?'

'Not really, no.'

'You lived next door. How did she strike you?'

'Oh dear. *De mortuis* . . . But I suppose murder cancels out not saying awful things about the dead. Well, I didn't like her. I thought she was pushy, arrogant, vain, snobbish, totally insensitive to other people's feelings – oh, and clever. What you might call multi-talented, all the social skills, as they called embroidery and such when they were fashionable. Including, I expect, the use of the globes, whatever that may be. It always reminds me of that Victorian picture of Mother showing Baby where Daddy is on the map of the world . . . you know.'

'Yes.' Sam didn't, but he thought Doran's reply a very fair one for a woman to make about someone she had loathed. 'Attractive, was she?'

'Very good-looking – she made the most of everything she had. She was the kind you meet when you feel you're looking a tramp yourself.'

'To men?'

'Well. Yes, I think. Her husband certainly adored her. And young Guy Culffe was crazy about her. Rupert Wylie . . .' She decided to tell Sam about Rupert and Paula on the night of the disappearance. 'That's all I know. It might have been quite innocent.'

'Makes passes at everybody, Mr Wylie, I seem to recall.'

Doran blushed. 'More or less.'

'Rodney? Did he find Mrs French attractive?'

'Couldn't stand her.' Surely Sam didn't include Rodney in his list of suspects? But he was saying something to the sergeant, obviously signing off the interview.

'Thank you, Doran. That's all been very helpful. We

shan't bother you any more unless we have to. Going to the shop today?'

'Yes, I think I will, I don't fancy this neighbourhood too much.'

Sam had seen the drawn look on Doran's face before. 'You go along now,' he said kindly, 'and don't think about this business if you can help it. Oh, just a minute, before you go – this man you said you glimpsed, just before you let yourself in here – what was his name, Ken Wedderbell? Tell me about him again.'

Doran told him about Ken Wedderbell.

'And the producer – Max . . . Johnston? What were his relations with Mrs French?'

'He loathed her. I think.' Doran told him of the scene that followed Paula's revelation of the red dress. 'He can be very angry. He just tolerated Paula, and he was obviously glad when – Tiggy – replaced her, even if it was going to be only temporary.'

'Any further incidents of Mr Johnston's flying into a rage?'

Doran hesitated. 'Not about Paula. I don't know whether I ought to tell you, Sam, I feel I'm peaching on everybody. Why don't you just ask them?'

'I will,' Sam returned mildly. 'I'm just getting your reactions, because it helps me to know things.'

'Oh, well. All right. I did notice Rupert getting fresh with Amy – Mrs Johnston – when they were doing the brother-and-sister duet, and I happened to see and hear a bit of a scene between them afterwards. And Max ignored Rupert as far as he could, the next evening. I suppose Amy had worked on him to keep the peace between them.'

Sam scribbled. 'And this was on the same night that Rupert Wylie took Mrs French to the woods?'

'Yes.'

'Did you see the Johnstons get into their car?'

'No.'

'So Max Johnston *could* have followed them?'

'Well . . . I suppose so. Don't take my word for anything, Sam.'

'I won't. Thanks, Doran.'

She saw, as she was starting up the car, other people arriving at the school. Max and Amy, Euan, Jack Turner. None of them looked happy, to say the least.

When she pulled up at the gate of Bell House an elegant little maroon car stood in its drive. Tiggy was loading the boot.

'Doran! I thought I might miss you. Is it over, I mean the Inquisition? Was it awful?'

'Not really, it was only Sam, but I'm glad it's over. You're not going, Tiggy? You can't!'

'Sorry, 'fraid I've got to. Nan rang me this morning and just *happened* to say that she'd had one of her turns, giddiness and fainting, you know how she is, won't admit to being ill, ever, but somehow it slipped out. So I said I'd go. You'll forgive me, won't you? Rodney says he'll hold the fort with Kit.'

'Yes, of course you must go.' Doran was struggling to take in the situation. Tiggy, leaving. Tiggy, who . . . She realized in the flash of a moment that by some freak of the mind the murder of Paula had cancelled out her own agonies over Tiggy and Rodney. She had thought they were in love, had been sure of it. Now, watching Tiggy in her very costly jeans, her hair fastened back in a workmanlike knot, fastening zips and pushing objects to the back of the boot, the whole thing seemed ridiculous, preposterous, a mad fancy.

'I've said goodbye to Kit, before he went to playschool. I don't think he quite took it in, poor child. Sorry about that. Now you're here I really think I'll start, you know what the roads are like this time of year. I said goodbye to Rodney in the house – now I'll say goodbye to you, and thank you a thousand million times for having me and letting me get to know Kit and drinking your gorgeous wine and simply *everything*.' A quick tight hug, a triple kiss Continental style, then the driver's door shut and Tiggy starting up the engine.

Then nothing, even the waving hand vanished round the corner of the lane. And Rodney appearing at the trellis gate, with a glass of beer.

'Want one?' he invited.

'Yes. Well, I don't know, I was going to the shop. It's awfully sudden, Tiggy leaving like that. Extraordinary, really.'

Rodney shrugged. 'There wasn't a lot for her to stay for, was there? The production's off now, of course, and I don't think she was much looking forward to it.' True, how true. 'If it had been still on I don't think her grandmother's turn would have weighed with her much.' Especially as it was fictitious.

Of course. For the first time Doran realized that *Yeomen* would never now take place. In the circumstances they couldn't possibly do it.

Sam was not enjoying his morning. With such a major crime, he felt sure that the Yard would involve itself very shortly. Usually possessive, like all local police, about his cases, he would positively welcome having this one taken off his hands.

Suspect Number One was the husband, as usual. Euan French seemed to Sam to be a broken man. And not surprising – but it made for unclear answers to questions.

'She was my sheet anchor, you see,' Euan said, not for the first time. 'I'm lost without her. I keep wondering how to re-make my life.'

'Yes, of course.' Sam could have said he understood only too well, as any devoted husband would. He felt the pain of it for Euan, and at one time would have said so freely. In his Abbotsbourne days nobody cruelly bereaved lacked for sympathy from the community constable. But experience in Eastgate had taught him just how much of himself he could expend on even the saddest case. It had been a tough lesson – even his wife thought (though she never said so) that it had hardened him. Yet it was necessary, if he was not to go to pieces under the stress of others' emotions. Professional turtles, programmed to hide behind armour: doctors, nurses, policemen, anyone whose job it was to deal with the suffering.

So, had the late Mrs French any enemies? Had there been a lover who might have turned jealous? When had Euan last seen her? Yes, he might have told someone already, but Sam needed to hear it again.

Euan shaded his eyes with his hand, as though his last picture of Paula rose in front of them.

'She was sitting . . . in the little room she used for sewing. She did a lot of that – our curtains, the chair-covers, things like that, as well as her clothes.'

Sam moved impatiently. 'Go on. Was she sewing then?'

Euan nodded. 'That red dress, the one there was so much fuss about. She was altering it, making it – quieter, I think she said. So that the others wouldn't go on about it.'

More accommodating than he'd gathered, Mrs French, Sam thought. Or cleverer, or very anxious to keep the part.

Euan saw the cynical flicker cross his interrogator's face.

'Don't think badly of her! She cared what they said about her. She realized that she'd gone too far with the costume. She was taking the spangles off it, throwing them into a box on the floor. Couldn't see what was wrong with it myself, it was so pretty.' His throat worked convulsively. 'I said didn't she know it was very late, and wouldn't it try her eyes, all those bright things under just a lamp, and no daylight. But she said she enjoyed working at night, when it was quiet. And she did, you know – she made that costume in two nights, with a rest after lunch. Wonderful! Don't you think so?'

'I've no idea. I know nothing about dressmaking. You were telling me about that evening. Did you say any more to your wife?'

'No. I just went to bed. I was pretty tired myself, and I sleep like a log.'

'So you can't say what time Mrs French went out?'

Euan shook his head, his eyes shut. Seeing things: the bright hair bent over the bright material. Sam could see it in his own mind, except that the hair kept changing into the grey curls of his wife Lydia.

'And next morning? What had she taken with her?'

'Nothing. Nothing. Nothing.'

'Oh, come, Mr French. There must have been something, unless your wife was abducted, which we don't think can have happened. Coat? Shoes? Handbag?'

'Everything she'd worn the night before. She's always so tidy, hanging things up and putting things in the linen-basket . . . But there was nothing. Just the bag and a summer raincoat gone. I don't know why she took that.'

Sam had seen the raincoat and the handbag, and something else.

'The red dress. It seems odd that she should have been wearing it. Why, do you think?'

Euan shuddered. 'I don't know.'

'Perhaps she tried it on after altering it, to see how she liked the effect.'

'Could be. Yes, she would have done. But why should she have . . . gone out? What happened, for God's sake?'

'We may know the answer to that when we've spoken to a few more people, Mr French. Now, that was definitely the last time you saw your wife – sewing. And you'd had no sort of disagreement – an argument, a quarrel? An atmosphere, even?'

Sergeant Dews reflected that it took a married man to interview one, in some ways.

'We never quarrelled. Neither of us was like that. You asked me that before.'

'I'm asking you again,' Sam said mildly, 'in case you've remembered something. About the hat.'

Euan looked at him, blank-eyed.

'The little – ' Sam consulted his notes. 'The little Tudor bonnet – so it's described here. With an imitation jewel and a feather.'

'I don't know. I didn't see it, then. It may have been there.'

It had not been there. It had been in the chest, the feather stained and stiffened, the mock gem lustreless. Somebody had a tidy mind.

Euan seemed to be struggling to speak. At last he managed it.

'Can I show you something?' He took out his wallet and spread the contents of one of its pouches on the table. They were all photographs, in colour, taken at various times and seasons, and all of Paula. Paula with her hair down, mermaid-style, looking provocatively through it. Paula in a bikini and huge pink shades, on a beach with an Italian-type harbour in the background. Paula in fancy dress, a medieval lady in a long brocade robe, sleeves of gold, a small hennin covering her hair, a light veil and a coronet. Paula indoors, laying her own dining table, an immaculate, welcoming TV commercial hostess. Paula smiling brilliantly, Paula pensive.

'Yes, I see. Thank you.' Sam handed the photographs back.

'I keep looking at them, you see. To remind me . . .' he choked.

Sam thought of Lydia, and wondered how safe the

suburbs of Eastgate were, whether somewhere there lurked a man with a grudge against him, Sam, which might be worked off, dreadfully, on Sam's wife. He dismissed Euan, thankful to feel the room empty of that oppressive grief.

The big Scotsman who was summoned next was a hostile witness from his entry. Max Johnston made it very clear that the police weren't getting any change out of him.

'Insult that woman? Ye couldn't insult her, she wouldn't listen long enough. Sure, I told her she was too old for the part, and when she'd the bloody nerve to turn up in that bloody awful tinsel dress I fired her, after I'd let her have a few home truths, such as she looked like an old-time hoor. Then that puir wimpish lad Guy hit me and the whole thing turned into a free-fight.' He described it, vividly, concluding with his own colourful views on two men daft enough to be deluded by the fading charms of such a lady.

'You didn't care for Mrs French, then?'

Max replied, with additions, that he did not, and that he would like to rejoin his wife immediately and take her back to London.

'I'm afraid we can't let you go quite yet.' Sam watched Max's face redden and his furry caterpillar eyebrows shoot up and down. A choleric man.

'But we have to get back. I don't need to be down here again till next month for the Festival, and Amy wants to go home, puir girl. She's suffered over this, I can tell ye.'

'Yes, I'm sure, Sir. But there are just a few more questions. Such as where you were on the night Mrs French disappeared?'

Max stared. 'Me?'

'Yes. The night of July eighteenth.'

'Why the devil should I tell you?'

'It's usual, during a police inquiry,' replied Sam

mildly. 'And I have reason to believe that you were not happy about Mr Wylie's conduct towards your wife at that rehearsal.'

After a few glares and time-wasting shufflings of his chair, Max condescended to admit that he'd been for a walk. He had no idea where, how the hell should he? He just wanted to work off his temper and Amy had begged him not to make a scene. All right, then, he'd gone over the Downs, somewhere with a lot of pointed hills that Doran had told him were hill forts. He hadn't met a soul, except for a sheep he fell over. It was late at night, why should anyone be up there? He saw nothing suspicious on his walk or when he got back to the hotel in Abbotsbourne. Why should he? Nobody chopping off anyone's head, for sure.

'And you didn't go back into the school that night, though I believe you may have had the key?'

'Aye. Some fool had left it sticking in the lock on the prop ring. But I just took it off and kept it. I didn't go back in. Why should I?'

Sam asked Amy, interviewed on her own, about the background to the lonely hill-walk – he felt he might get more out of her, you generally did with an emotional woman. Amy's pretty face showed signs of tears and stress. Her big eyes, made up today almost to stage requirements, were the eyes of a mournful Mary Magdalen, a part she had once sung with great effect. But at least she was not crying or hysterical.

'Max often goes off for walks when we're staying in the country,' she told them. 'We're so cooped up in the flat in London, with no garden, only a little balcony, and Max has such long legs and needs more exercise. Besides, that night – '

'Yes?'

Amy looked down at her hands, twisting her wedding ring, which was very bright and fairly new. 'Well. There'd been some trouble, words, a bit of fighting, in fact, at the rehearsal the night before. Someone didn't like what Max said to Mrs French, and hit him, and then someone else joined in, and it was all a bit messy. I did say to Max that he'd gone a bit too far.'

'These someones were Guy Culffe and his sister, I believe?'

'Well, yes. And when I came to work that old spinning wheel I *knew* why there was wickedness in the air. Though Mrs Evans said she thought it wasn't the spinning wheel but the chest where . . .' She shuddered. 'She might have been right, I don't know. My instincts usually tell me.'

'So,' Sam continued patiently, 'your husband was still disturbed by the scene which had taken place at the previous rehearsal.'

'Yes.' A faint look of relief crossed Amy's face.

'And nothing else – say, some familiarity on the part of Mr Wylie, in your duet?'

Amy blushed hotly.

'How did you know? Oh dear. Yes, as a matter of fact. Rupert got a bit fresh during the duet where he has to kiss me – very fresh, really. I didn't like it at all. Max didn't notice at the time but when I told him afterwards he was furious, livid, he said he'd do all sorts of things to Rupert. But I managed to calm him down, though he was still simmering when we got back to the hotel. I said it was nothing, Rupert was like that with all the women, and I'd give him a thorough brush-off at the next rehearsal. But Max said he still felt churned up and he'd have to go for a walk. And he did.'

Her candid gaze held no guile, Sam was sure. She obviously loved and cherished her husband very much, as he did her. Whatever sinister had happened that night, he would never have burdened her with it. Nor would she have betrayed him, had she known anything.

'Nice lady,' commented Sergeant Dews when she had gone.

'Very.' Sam too liked them ultra-feminine, delicate creatures to be protected.

Rupert Wylie was furious at being questioned.

'None of it's to do with me. I wish I'd never got mixed up with their rotten production. Having it in the papers isn't going to do the firm much good, I can tell you, and you can bet they won't miss it, the county papers and the freerag on top of the nationals – junior partner in Dixter and Wylie, Abbotsbourne's leading estate agents, questioned in Headless Woman case.'

'I don't think – ' began Sam.

'Might be Wylie and Wylie some day, if my wife throws a boy this time, and what would it look like to him, his dad accused of . . .'

'We're not accusing you of anything, Mr Wylie. I merely think you're not being entirely frank with me. Now come along – I think everybody knows you're fond of the ladies. I just want to know how well you knew Mrs French. Did you ever flirt with her – have any sort of relationship?'

'Polite language you coppers use. No, I didn't. I didn't even fancy her. It was just that one time – but it wasn't really anything.'

'I think you'd better tell me.'

'Well. It was a hot night, and hot weather always has that effect on me – *you* know.' He gave Sam a portentous wink. 'I hadn't had much luck, one way and another – didn't expect Amy to be that difficult, I mean she's not a youngster, is she, you'd think she'd had plenty of experience.'

Sam saw that Dews was writing busily. He wondered how his sergeant was expressing the evidence.

'But no, not a bit of it,' Rupert continued. 'I was fed up, and when I saw old Paula sort of frittering about on her own I grabbed her and said come for a walk.

She said something or other about getting a hat she'd left in the school, but I persuaded her out of that, and we went up in the woods.'

'And?'

Rupert shrugged. 'She stood me up, didn't she. Or not, if you see what I mean. She just thought it was a laugh, leading me on. I could have bashed her – but I didn't, if that's what you're thinking.' He shuddered. 'I called her a few names and went back to my car. Never saw her again. Don't know where she went. When I left her she was laughing like a drain. Is that all?'

'For the moment. But I'd be glad if you'll stay in the district until we've made all our inquiries, Mr Wylie. If you have to leave it for professional purposes please give us an address where you can be reached.'

Sam watched him leave. Detachedly he admired Rupert. A fine physical specimen.

'Truthful, would you say, Dews?'

'I should think so, sir. Not much imagination.'

'That's what I thought. And a knocker-down, rather than an axeman?'

Hugo Snaresby was obviously a stuffy man with a professional reputation to guard. It was difficult to visualize him risking it for a woman, or turning violent if rejected. Likewise Ralph Chapman, a respected figure in Abbotsbourne church life, already under censure by his vicar for taking part in an Elvesham activity. The bank man, Alex Warner, seemed a spiritless creature who had never previously been involved in anything of the kind, and seemed to have no fixed personality. None of these three looked strong enough to have struck the blow. Sam thought it as well that *Yeomen* was to be scrapped, if they were reduced to casting such people. None of the three middle-aged men seemed to have any strong views on the late Paula.

Jack Turner was very reluctant to be interviewed at

all. He protested that it was taking him away from his shop where his son couldn't be expected to cope alone and his wife wasn't properly trained to serve. He wished he had never got mixed up with the whole business.

'Only did it for the sake of my old dad, and if he's lookin' down on us he'll be right vexed to see his son in a mess like this. I wish I'd never touched the blasted chopper. I only thought it'd look better on the stage.'

'How did you feel about Mrs French?'

Turner glowered. 'I didn't like her.'

'Why?'

'Complained about cuts of meat – had the nerve to come into my shop and show me a diagram of the parts of a pig – *me*! Preached at me about cookery. *And* in front of a shopful of customers. Enough to get me a bad name. No, I couldn't stand the woman.'

'But you could have killed her. You've had experience of a slaughter-house. You'd know just where to strike.'

The butcher's face was crimson with wrath. 'What do you know about it? Let me tell you . . .' He launched into a grisly account of various methods practised in slaughter-houses, which Sam had inspected in his time, but which he had tried to put out of his mind, though Doran had told him this was hypocrisy, and if he felt like that he ought to become a vegetarian. Sergeant Dew's face relaxed its impassivity to show distaste.

Sam got rid of Jack Turner curtly, for him. He took a long drink of water, wishing it were beer.

'No use talking to the chorus,' he said to Dews. 'They haven't been called yet, the orchestra rehearsals weren't due to start until Monday. I'm knocking off now, and I suggest you do. Tell Fox not to talk to anyone, press or public. It's too late for lunch now, but I suppose we can get some tea and food on the way back to Eastgate to take some more statements. Oh – just a minute, I've a call to make. Get me this number.'

Doran answered.

'Sam! Yes, I'm still at the shop. Have you – all this time? You poor thing. Yes, of course I'll meet you somewhere. Port Arms? No, too many people we know. Just a minute, Howell's saying something.'

The telephone went dead as she pressed the silence button which cuts out the person making the call from the muffled conversation going on at the other end. Then he heard her again.

'Howell kindly says will we go to Reefers – his house – and give ourselves a drink or some tea – he and Gwenllian are going out. Good idea? All right. See you.'

Before he locked up Sam said to his sergeant, 'Now you go over to Barminster and see what's keeping young Mr Culffe and his sister, will you? If they turn awkward on you, bring them in.'

10

Oh, woe is me, I rather think

The parlour at Reefers was as benevolently welcoming as ever. Marie Antoinette simpered majestically in Parian ware, a Regency bracket clock in the shape of a lyre was new to Doran, and evidence to her that Howell's taste was broader than he would readily admit: it looked prepared to play 'The Bluebells of Scotland' on the next hour.

The lace draping on the chaise-longue had been replaced by a very beautiful Indian silk shawl in tulip colours, and the walnut square piano had disappeared altogether, replaced by a pretty inlaid cabinet-on-stand, which would have displeased perfectionists because its long turned legs were two centuries younger than its body. It would be absorbed into the trade when Howell had stopped being amused by it.

Sam had not been in Howell's cottage before. To his eyes it looked tatty and overcrowded, but his taste was not that of Doran's friend. He was more interested in the pleasant cool draught that came from the back window opening on to a small patio, even though the security angle worried him slightly.

Doran removed the shawl and stretched out on the chaise-longue, undoing another button of her dress. The dress was of pale primrose cotton: Sam thought it made her look colourless and washed out, though he fancied that the shadow of grief or anxiety he had seen over her that morning had lightened faintly.

'That's pretty.' He nodded towards a Berlin plaque of a girl's face peeping smilingly from a red hood. 'I bet you could tell me all about it, how much it's worth and so on.'

'I could, but I won't. You didn't ask me to meet you to discuss porcelain. What is it? Something I can do to help?'

Sam sighed deeply. 'You know those cases where the Yard call in Mr Holmes, or Dr Thorndyke or some other amateur, and ask for their advice. Hard to credit, I always find that.'

'So do I. I believe much more in the detective-inspector or whatever who turns pale at the approach of Miss Marple and mutters "Nosey old ferret" to his sergeant. Do I take it you're in the unlikely behaviour corner?'

Sam smiled, without mirth. 'I'm in the corner where the Yard's going to move in with me any minute, and if I'm right about who they'll send, your advice won't be welcome. That's why I'm talking to you, before he gets here. I've seen all the witnesses now, bar the ones at Eastgate, and I'm no farther on, in fact I'm lost. I can't believe any of 'em did it. So I'm asking you, off the record, if you've got any instincts.'

'Sam, Sam. Female intuition isn't permitted by the rules of the Detection Club. Anyway, I haven't got any about any of them. I've been a bit preoccupied, actually.'

'Kit?'

'Something to do with him, yes – but he's all right. There's just one thing – did Max Johnston strike you as a very angry man?'

'He used pretty violent language about the dead lady, yes.'

'Mm. Do you know, Sam, I think his anger's really directed at himself. He rejected Paula for the part of Elsie at the audition, then let her talk him into changing his mind. Now he's kicking himself for being such a fool – and I shouldn't be surprised if it hasn't occurred to him that this whole ghastly business mightn't have happened, if he'd stuck to his first decision.'

'That's interesting. What about you, Doran? Do *you* think it wouldn't have happened?'

Doran was taking the lid off a silver Art Deco cigarette box and putting it on, absently.

'I think Paula was the sort of person who'd have been murdered eventually,' she said, 'given enough provocation to the other party.'

'Why?'

'Because she always knew best.'

Before Sam could answer, the door from the staircase opened and Gwenllian Evans's head looked out.

'Ah,' she said, emerging fully, 'the very man.' She was wearing a lace dress of Tyrian purple with a sequinned peacock climbing up it, dark green stockings and a long rope of multi-coloured beads. She went up to Sam and clasped his hand warmly.

'We met last night, you remember?'

Sam said he remembered, wondering how she could possibly expect anyone to forget. She touched Doran's shoulder lightly in the manner of a queen impulsively bestowing an accolade, and perched herself on a chair.

'Well now. Detective-Inspector, is that right, or have I promoted you or the other way round? I always do get these things wrong. I'm told you wanted to see me and ask me questions, so here I am. Oh, I know I ought to be at this party affair in somebody's garden looking at statues with Hywel, but what's a party when you're wanted by the Law?'

'I wouldn't put it quite like that, Mrs Evans,' said Sam, 'but it's very nice of you. Thoughtful. In fact, as you'd never met the deceased lady and only attended a rehearsal after she'd disappeared from the scene, there's only one main question I want to ask you.'

Gwenllian waited, her jetty head tilted, a blackbird hearing a luscious worm stirring in the ground.

'I understand that when you were first introduced to Mrs Chelmarsh and the disappearance of Mrs French was discussed, you suggested that she might have been murdered. Can you tell me what made you think that?'

The blackbird savoured the worm. 'I've seen it happen, you know. A woman, no chicken, old enough to know her onions – very much the sort some gentlemen fancy, others take a hate to her because she's stronger than them – women, well, they hate her, don't they, she's a rival, whether they're girls or old ladies like me. So if they bump into her when they happen to have a knife in their hand – or it might be an axe, they – ' She slashed her fingers across her throat.

'Yes, I see. Thank you. And you were the second person to see the body, after Mrs Chelmarsh. Did it shock you?'

'I was brought up rough,' Gwenllian said after a little pause. 'Some hard types come in on the boats. And our men, in those days they'd go to Chap-el Sunday morning, but Saturday nights, some of them'd get fighting drunk. My man was one.'

'I know,' said Doran before she could stop herself. She'd heard of the wife-beating drunk who had been Howell's father, but until now the mother-figure of his childhood had been unreal to her. The reality of Howell's mother explained a lot about him. Why he turned to youths who were neither all man nor all woman, why he had within him a spring of fighting blood, why a part of him held the fatherly tenderness his own father had not shown him, why he had had to raise himself from back-street level and become a hard, shrewd bargainer with a streak of dishonesty. She knew all the reasons now.

Sam's thoughts were only on the murder. 'You've had experience of violence, Mrs Evans, I can see that.

But what I asked you was whether the sight of . . . a corpse murdered in that way shocked you.'

'Now there's a silly question, if I may say so.' Gwenllian's brilliant eyes were hidden, secret. 'I seen men brought up from the mines after an explosion. I was young and inquisitive, so I looked, though nobody was meant to. After that I can take a woman with her head off. Can I go now? There's some nice lemonade in the fridge, Doran, I made it myself, if the Detective-whateffer isn't drinking on duty.'

When she had gone Sam said, 'That's a funny woman.'

'Ha-ha or peculiar?'

'Both. I can't help wondering why a crime like this should follow as soon as she moves into the neighbourhood.'

'Oh, come, Sam, be reasonable. It isn't the first time she's stayed with Howell, by any means – she just didn't happen to come up to Abbotsbourne or Elvesham, that's all. Whatever else she is, I'm sure she isn't a murderess.'

Sam grunted. 'I'd like to know a bit more about her, that's all. By the way, you shouldn't have been in on that, Doran.'

Doran widened her eyes innocently. 'I didn't see you taking an official statement.'

'No, because I wasn't. Dews ought to have been here. I'm making a mess of this.' He turned full to her, the bright sunshine that streamed through the window showing up every line, every downward drag of his facial muscles, the increasing greyness of his neat moustache. 'I'm getting past this game,' he said.

Yes, it was true, the saying about the policemen getting younger as one got older. Ambition had never been part of Sam's make-up. To be community cop at Abbotsbourne had suited him perfectly, with its comparatively light work programme, the most awful face

of crime usually turned away from him. He had lived the life of a villager, though with special responsibilities, preoccupying himself with his family, his garden, his friends and neighbours, and his beloved church bells, his Ladies in the Tower: Evangelist, the treble, Sancta Maria, the second bell, Jacobus the third, Saint Paul the fourth, Jesu the fifth, and Great Harry the tenor. Bells, like ships, were always spoken of as female. Their old inscriptions were engraved on his memory. *Sancta Maria ora pro nobis, Sancte Paula ora pro animam meam, Jesu est amor meus* . . . All far distanced from Eastgate nick and ugly murders.

Hastily Doran switched her glance, uncomfortably aware that their long closeness of spirit was keeping them in silent communication now, and that was not good for Sam.

'No, I shouldn't have been in on that. Never mind, officially I wasn't, I just happened to be in the room when the witness entered. That sounds all right, doesn't it? And as I rather want to be there when you take statements from your next witnesses, I think I'll do a further bit of happening – if it's all right with you. You'd better write up your notes on Mrs Evans, though.'

Sam patted her shoulder gratefully. Doran understood, and when the time came for him to retire gracefully his wife Lydia would understand, and his little daughter Jennifer. He hoped, earnestly, that he would not do a Blue Lamp before that time arrived by getting himself knocked off on duty.

The next witness to be visited was Meg. She was sitting crosslegged on a table that passed for a counter, sewing in the way of an old-style tailor. As Sam sat down beside her Doran faded tactfully away behind a rack of clothes, making herself technically invisible.

Meg was prepared for the visit, and full of her own views.

'. . . I hardly knew the woman, of course, not going to Abbotsbourne all that much, but what I saw of her at rehearsals I didn't care for a lot. It was absolutely not done and rotten of her to turn up in that red dress, making a spectacle of herself when she could see with half an eye that none of the rest of us could afford anything like that – and anyway it didn't fit in with the rest of the wardrobe. I know she altered it a bit, but the whole thing was unsuitable.'

Sam had heard a good deal about the red dress, had even seen it, though not at its best.

'I shouldn't wonder,' Meg mused, 'if somebody killed her because of that dress.'

'Oh? Could you expand a bit on that?'

'No, I don't think I could.' Meg snapped off a thread. 'It was just that it caused so much bad feeling. Max was furious about it, Amy was upset, though she didn't say much, because it was going to show her Phoebe costume up so much. Ruth was livid, I shouldn't be surprised if it didn't help to make her ill, she was in such a temper. Rupert, well . . .' She lowered her voice to a whisper, which Doran managed to hear. 'I think it made him a bit – *you* know, like he gets with women – because when I was unlocking the car to go home I saw him with Doran, er, trying to start something. Oh dear, I shouldn't have told you that.'

'Quite allowable as evidence,' Sam said. 'Anything else, Mrs Rye?'

This time Meg didn't bother to whisper.

'I just wondered how it affected Guy Culffe, that's all. He got so terribly worked up in that fight when he hit Max, and he's such a peculiar boy. I thought it might have excited him – in another way, if you see what I mean. Paula would have noticed that, and she was a bit of a tease, you know . . .'

'Yes.' Sam was writing busily, angry with himself because he had sent Dews away instead of keeping him to take statements. Dews would just have to copy his own and get them put on computer at the nick that night.

He called Doran over. 'This next bit is where you come in, Doran. Another Eastgate resident, Mr Ken Wedderbell, seen in Elvesham just before you found the body. I think we'd better talk to him. If we could ask your husband for directions, Mrs Rye – '

'Oh yes. Peg's out sketching – he sells watercolours, you know – I can tell you exactly where to find him.'

Peg was in the old fishing quarter, on the beach at his easel, painting the strange tall net-sheds. He used his watercolours delicately, laying the brown of the timber against the robin's-egg blue of the sky that mirrored itself in the calm Channel, emphasizing among the children playing on the beach the scarlet of a red towelling wrap, catching the wet bobbing heads of swimmers like bubbles on the surface of the sea. Such a quaint, absurd little man, thought Doran, yet so much talent, a natural English watercolourist . . .

Sam's voice brought Doran back to the real world, asking Peg if he could possibly break off long enough to direct them to Wedderbell's house. An artist less good-natured might well have grumbled, working as he was in perfect weather conditions, but Peg just said, 'Of course.'

Sam's cluttered boot managed to contain the folding easel and painting materials. He knew the streets of Eastgate backwards, so that Peg's directions were hardly necessary. In a few minutes they were in the run-down square, looking up at the sad terraced house and the sign glued to the inside of a downstairs window.

'I'll handle this,' Sam said. 'In case there's any trouble.'

His relentless ringing of each bell finally produced the opening of a bedroom window on the first floor. A female head appeared, asking crossly what the 'ell they wanted.

'Police,' Sam answered. 'I'd like a word with Mr Wedderbell.'

'Not seen 'im for days. Nothing to do with me.'

'He still lives here, I suppose?'

'Dunno. 'Ear 'im sometimes, but not for a day or two. Three, maybe.'

'May I come in and have a word?'

'No, yer can't, I'm busy.' The window was slammed down.

'Well, that's that. Back to the nick for a search warrant.' Sam's shoulders drooped. Doran was sorry for him. For once she would like to have been a WPC and taken over from him, so that he could go home.

'You don't really think he's been up to anything – like what's happened?' Peg asked. 'He's just a weedy beat-up wreck with a bottle problem. I can't see him tackling a fit woman, can you, Doran?'

Doran said she could believe a limitless number of impossible things about anyone before breakfast or at any other time.

They deposited Peg and his painting gear at the net-sheds, though the lovely late afternoon light was beginning to change, and Sam wearily set off back to the nick, Doran accompanying him, by her own request. She too was tired, but anxious not to have time to think. About anything.

Armed with the warrant, they got into the house through a back door, opened by the unwelcoming middle-aged tenant of the first floor.

There was no sign of Wedderbell in the double drawing room crammed with treasures, and no alteration that Doran could see in the treasures themselves. Down the dark dangerous stairs the same dank, stuffy smell prevailed, but nothing more sinister. Between them they opened everything capable of containing a human body – chests, cupboards, presses, even longcase clocks. Behind a pile of chairs Doran found an unnoticeable door, pushed away the chairs and turned a stiff Bakelite handle. She looked in and shut the door hastily.

'A loo,' she said. 'Not appetizing.'

'Talking of appetite, what about food, a kitchen? He must have one.'

It was beyond the stairs, a dark cupboard of a room with a card-table, a chair, and a stone sink containing unwashed china. There was no way of telling how long it might be since anyone had eaten there, although the milk in an almost-empty bottle had gone very sour. A camp-bed had been roughly made up with stale sheets.

Sam sighed. 'All right. I'll go and put him on the computers. I've got to see if anything's come in from Dews at Barminster, about young Culffe. You push off home, Doran.'

Doran started to say something, but stopped herself. Sam had had nearly enough. And so had she.

'You can't come in. I've told you once.'

People seldom argued with Maggie Culffe when she stated anything firmly. She was sober and not in the mood for trifling.

Neither was Sergeant Dews, that stony-faced young man with a chin that looked sharp enough to cut open someone's hand, if rashly struck. His foot was just far enough inside the doorsill to prevent her shutting him out of her shop. After a silent battle of wills, and Maggie's own abandonment of her impulse to give him a violent push backwards, she let him in.

'I'm shut, anyway.' She reversed the Open-Shut card on the inside of the door. 'And how do I know you're what the card says you are? Things like that can be forged.'

'If you'd examine the photograph, madam.' But he

knew that she had already taken in his likeness – she was just being obstructive.

In the back room, something between an office, store-room and sitting room, she reluctantly took a chair and watched him do the same. His sharp eyes, not seeming to move from his notebook and recorder, were everywhere. Bottles in the filing cabinet, he reckoned. Glass-rim stains on the table top. An unmistakable whiff of scotch. He asked her all the questions, his eyes looking a little past her, where she sat in the full light from the window, a short, heavily built woman with a complexion coarsened by drink. Dews was not susceptible to the charms of female witnesses, and he was equally unaffected by the lack of charms in this one.

No, she hadn't particularly liked Paula French, though she didn't know her well enough to say. She thought Paula had spoken nicely to her brother Guy after the producer had been so rude to him. The man was a swine, anyway.

Yes, she had backed Guy up after his attack on Max Johnston. She was very angry and thought he deserved punishment for treating a woman like that. They had gone straight home and Guy had been very upset.

It seemed to come as a surprise to her to be asked if she would have attacked Paula, in the case of Paula treating her brother badly.

'Why should she treat him badly? He thought she was attractive, yes. But Guy would never have done anything to – to provoke her. He admired her, she must have been flattered by that. Nonsense, the whole suggestion.'

'I'll have to question Mr Culffe personally, madam.'

Maggie moved rapidly to the door and stood with her back against it.

'You can't. He's ill, he's been off work.'

'I know that, madam. I'm afraid I must still speak to him.'

They fought out a battle of wills. At last Maggie shrugged, opened the door, and started up the stairs from the shop to the living quarters, throwing over her shoulder, 'You'll have to keep your voice down, he's in a very nervous state and I think he's got a temperature. Really, we could have done without this . . .'

The small bedroom was very much a boy's room, Dews thought, not a young man's. The pop posters on the wall were dated. A model plane, made from a kit, stood on the window sill. Framed photographs stood about, a lot of girls, a woman probably Guy's mother. The furniture was G-plan, bought by somebody else, Dews guessed. A few magazines of the girlie sort were piled on a table. Dews examined them. Nothing particularly hot, just a lot of displays of what were known to Dews and his contemporaries as B. and T. Paperbacks in something that was hardly a bookcase – sex and crime, the sort Dews read himself when he read anything.

The boy on the bed was still wearing shirt and trousers as Dews discovered by throwing back the bedclothes, not heeding Maggie's protest. Guy was lying in the foetal position, curled up, arms crossed. Not meeting Dews's eyes, he turned his face and buried it in the pillows.

'Now, Mr Culffe. Perhaps you'll tell me a few things. You seemed to take Mrs French's death pretty hard. Why was that?'

An inarticulate sound, and a shudder of the shoulders. What Dews could see of Guy's face was scarlet, and wet, whether with tears or sweat it was impossible to say. Insistently the policeman's questions went on, extracting no answer. He touched the shoulder nearest to him, and instantly Guy turned over, rolling away to the limit of the narrow bed, and began to make a feeble, repetitive moaning sound. Maggie put her arm protectively across her brother, her own face crimson with anger.

'Leave him alone, will you? Can't you see he's not fit for questions? Anyway, what have you got against him – why shouldn't he be upset by a nasty murder like that?'

Dews, whose strongest weapon was silence, put away his notebook, gave one more long, considering look at the bed, and left the room. Behind him he heard Maggie murmuring, soothing. He let himself out. Back in his car he spoke to Sam at Eastgate.

'Nothing to be got out of young Culffe, sir. Shamming illness, it looks like. Sister won't give, either. Follow up inquiries, sir?'

Rodney had expected trouble when one of the helpful young mothers had brought Kit back from play-school. Finding his father alone in the kitchen, painstakingly preparing lunch, his first question was, 'Where's Tiggy, Daddy?'

Rodney took a deep breath. 'I'm afraid she had to go, Kit.'

'Oh. Will she be long?'

'Er, yes. In fact she's not coming back. Her grandmother isn't well, so she's had to go to Brighton to be with her. She sent you lots of love and said she was sorry she couldn't wait till you got back, and she'll come and see you again as soon as she can. Perhaps when her grandmother's better.'

The corners of Kit's mouth turned down and his chin began to quiver, the enormity of the event beginning to get to him. In his short life he had suffered one major loss already, the going of Helena. Though he had forgotten with his conscious mind, there was an ache somewhere below the surface, ready to awake and hurt. His father and mother had given him emotional security. Neither of them had ever threatened to go away and leave him. On the whole, he liked most people. But Tiggy had given him something he had never known before, even from Helena's obsessive love, the concentrated attention and care of someone who thoroughly understood children and especially him, her friends' little son, and a warmth that he recognized even at his young age as being a particular feeling between female and male. It had sown the seeds of a future susceptibility and tenderness towards pretty, kindly women who were not one's mother, pretty and kindly though she was, too. Mummy was Mummy, and a great important part of his life. But Tiggy was special.

He burst into tears. Rodney abandoned the lunch and took his son on his lap.

'Oh, Kitten, don't. It's all right, it's all right. It couldn't be helped . . . Here, have my hankie. It couldn't be helped . . .'

With such ineffectual comforts he tried to stem Kit's grief. But Kit, not usually a crybaby, very brave about physical hurt, would not be comforted. At last Rodney gave up, and let him cry himself into exhaustion, lying on the floor where he had thrown himself, his sobs punctuated by gulps of 'I want Tiggy'.

A massive understatement, thought Rodney. But you'll get over it. I have the worse burden of knowing it was my sin that led to your grief. I deserve all I feel now, which is a lot. It is a fearful thing to fall into the hands of the living God, and I have done just that. I never have believed in Purgatory, and after this I shall believe in it even less. Purgatory is here and now, the voice in the mind telling one, the – all right, television screen – in the mind, showing one the wrong done, the hurt and betrayal inflicted. But I am a priest, still. I've been shown the way, given the password. *Keep innocency, and take heed unto the thing that is right; for that shall bring a man peace at the last.*

When Kit had quietened enough to drink some milk and eat a slice of bread and honey, Rodney said, 'Come on, we're going for a walk.'

The curls so like Doran's were shaken violently. 'Don't want to.'

'Well, I do, and I think you ought to keep me company. Get up. That's the way.'

Holding Kit's warm damp hand firmly, and chatting of this and that, Rodney led him the short way to the church. The door had been left unlocked, perhaps because of the heat, though it was not like Edwin Dutton to expose its treasure to possible riflers.

'Now,' he said, 'you don't really know this place awfully well, do you, because Mrs Dutton tells stories to you lot in the little room outside.' (It had displaced a number of ancient and interesting graves, and Rodney thoroughly objected to it, but this was not the moment to pass on such views.)

'It's a very interesting church if you really look at it. Who's that, up in that window?'

'Jesus,' replied Kit mechanically.

'No, for once it isn't. It's a man called Thomas Carlyle, pretending to be King Saul in the Bible.'

'And 'n angel.'

'No, that's a boy called David playing the harp. They called him the sweet singer of Israel, because his music made people feel better. And those other rather odd-looking gentlemen in antique clothing are Mr Gladstone and Mr Disraeli and Lord Salisbury. I've always thought this was the ideal stained-glass window to distract a wandering mind from the sermon. You'll understand all about that one day.' If they still preached sermons then.

Kit appeared still very subdued, but generally drier. Rodney led him to the reredos in the south aisle, a gem of alabaster carving, and found a complex and quite inaccurate explanation for St Catherine's wheel and the attack on St Thomas à Becket by four knightly assassins. This last seemed to cheer Kit up considerably. He was even persuadable to play round the table tomb of a thirteenth-century de Brassey, where he could do no foreseeable harm. There were twelve weepers, miniature figures of the departed's heirs and mourners, ranged in line on one side, and an interesting heraldic beast of no known species curled at the effigy's feet. Rodney, ears alert for trouble, wandered off towards the altar of the church that had once been his.

When Doran's car turned in at the gate of Bell House that evening Rodney was standing at the window. He felt spiritually restored, curiously light-hearted and cheerful.

Doran kissed him, as she always did on coming home. In her depleted state she at once sensed the change in him. Jack Point and his woes were gone: Rodney was back.

'Should you ask me what kind of day I've had,' she said, 'and you've got a few hours to spare, I'll tell you. Preferably over supper, but I don't suppose we've got much, with Tiggy deserting the ship like that.'

'Oddly enough, we have. I made a quiche, the way Tiggy showed me last week, and it really wasn't difficult. You take some eggs and mushrooms and onions – oh, well, you know, of course. And I found some frozen pastry. Kit liked his bit of it, anyway. I made a lot and washed some salad.'

Doran gave him an extra kiss. 'You're marvellous. But don't turn into Man with Apron, it isn't your image. I meant to buy something cooked to have tonight, then I forgot, but it wouldn't have been as nice as yours will be.'

She looked round the neat drawing room. It had, like Rodney, reverted to normal.

'I thought I'd miss Tiggy,' she said. 'But somehow,

I'm quite glad she's gone, and we're on our own again. If you don't find it too boring,' she added carefully.

'Quite the reverse. I wouldn't go all the way with Sam Johnson and his "Fish and guests stink in three days", but I know what he meant. Disturbing influences. However charming.'

'Right.'

Nothing more was said: dare be said.

The quiche was a trifle overdone but delicious. Over it, Rodney said, 'Nothing will persuade me you've been at the shop all afternoon. Any developments about Paula?'

'Nothing.' She told him the substance of the day's investigations.

'Poor Paula. No motives, no regrets, it seems, except from Guy and Euan – I'll go round and see him after supper.'

'Good. We haven't thought enough about *her*, poor thing. Whatever she was like, she can't have deserved *that*.'

'I went into church this afternoon – Kit was a bit piney, and I thought it would divert him. I'd have lit a candle for Paula, but of course Edwin's thrown them out along with the other High trimmings. I . . . said a few words, in lieu.'

'I'm glad.'

'On the principle of *Orate pro anima Hamilton Tighe*.'

They remembered their unofficial Ingoldsby honeymoon. Doran's hand went out to Rodney's but before they could touch the telephone rang.

'Oh Malachi!' exclaimed Rodney. (It had become his practice to swear by the Prophets since Kit's arrival, as being forceful but never blasphemous.) 'The press again.'

A national this time, asking for a quote from the elusive Mrs Chelmarsh.

*

Next morning Sam, arriving at the Barminster shop to pursue inquiries, found an hysterical Maggie Culffe trying to revive Guy from a barbiturate-induced coma. A suicide note was beside him.

11

Oh! my brother

The local radio announcer revealed as much as police sources had disclosed to his news desk, the latest snippet in the fascinating case of the Elvesham Murder. A witness in the case had been taken to hospital in a coma. When he recovered consciousness the police hoped he would be able to help them in their inquiries.

'Guy,' said Doran. 'It has to be. Oh, that wretched boy.'

'It ought to have been me,' said Euan. He was sharing their breakfast at Bell House, brought home the previous night by Rodney, who had been concerned at his spending another night of lonely grief in his own home, with its constant reminders of Paula.

Doran sympathized, but was increasingly unsure that it had been a good idea. Euan had wakened them all in the small hours, screaming in a nightmare, and Kit had been difficult to get to sleep again. Breakfast, normally a cheerful meal accompanied by Rodney's comments on his propped-up newspaper, had been an uneasy affair of tempting Euan's poor appetite and making conversation.

'I'd have been no trouble to you then,' Euan said miserably. 'Or to anyone, especially myself. I ought to have done it, it's so easy, they say. Just a handful of tablets and a few drinks. Then nothing. Only we don't know there's nothing, do we? That's why I'd be too frightened.'

'Hamlet made much the same observations,' Rodney

remarked. 'It's a line of thought I'd advise you to abandon, Euan. No good to anyone.'

'I can't forget it for a minute, you see. Everywhere I look, she's there. The mirrors are worst. I used to brush her hair for her, when she wore it long.'

'Yes, very natural,' Doran put in hurriedly, glad that Kit had asked to get down from table early. She found herself adding, 'Of course, you can stay here as long as you like.' She hadn't meant to say it, didn't mean it. Rodney's face gave away his shock-horror reaction. Euan brightened.

'Do you really mean that? Oh yes, please, if you can put up with me.'

Doran did some lightning thinking. 'You *could* try the Rose, of course. It would be, er, further away, less of a constant reminder.'

Euan shook his head. 'No, I wouldn't like that, I'd have to face people all the time. I just need you and this lovely happy home. If you knew how I envy you, Rodney . . .' His face crumpled.

Rodney folded his unread paper and rose. 'I know how you feel. I envy me, too, so to speak. Now, if you'll forgive me, I have to go and finish off a thing for Dela to catch the post.' Doran exchanged looks with him as he went out.

He was waiting for her in the dining room, where his Radio Dela material was kept, but it had not been laid out on the table.

'I'm sorry, so sorry,' she said. 'What a fool I was, blurting that out! It's the kind of thing one says but doesn't mean for a moment. I couldn't bear it for long.'

'Nor could I, I'm afraid. Nor Kit – children catch emotions, like germs. I should be ashamed to own it. When I was living in that awful vicarage I used to have to take distressed people in for the night, sometimes, but it's never happened here, and I don't want it. I meant last night to be strictly a one off, he was in such a state when I went round. I tried a touch of spiritual consolation, but he didn't seem interested. And now we've got ourselves a lodger.'

'In severe depression.'

'Odd,' Rodney mused, 'the British attitude to hospitality. In America, I hear, they fling wide the gates, kill any fatted calves that happen to be passing, and offer you the half of their kingdom. Whereas the Englishman stands in front of his cave and snarls.'

This particular Englishman hadn't done that in the case of Tiggy, Doran reflected.

'Well, we've got to unload Euan – poor thing. Soon. But now I have to ring Sam.'

Sam was not on duty, the Eastgate desk informed her. The Elvesham murder investigation was now in the hands of Chief Inspector Ogle of Scotland Yard.

'That man,' she burst out to Rodney. 'My evil genius, he is. The bane of Abbotsbourne when all that Mumbray business was going on, then he turns up at Caxton Manor with his hatchet profile twitching – and now he's moved in here.'

'As Assistant Tormentor.'

'Yes, and he *likes* Assistant Tormenting, which is more than Shadbolt said he did. He's going to mean trouble, you see.'

'I thought we had trouble already,' said Rodney mildly.

Chief Inspector Ogle would not have admitted that he liked Assistant Tormenting, or any other variety, though he felt with modest pride that the interrogation of witnesses brought out the best in him. He loved in particular to jump on people with questions they weren't expecting.

His single-minded keenness had not gone unnoticed by his superiors – he had seen to that. It had won him promotion and New Scotland Yard, though not the large desk and wall-to-wall carpeting he had envisioned. He had also been pained to find himself up against men even harder-nosed than himself who had dented his self-complacency in various nasty ways. All the more he welcomed the opportunity to return to the Abbotsbourne region, where he had felt very much at home among the simple natives. True, he hadn't been conspicuously successful in tracking down the murderer in either local case in the past, but there had been so many eccentrics involved that he could hardly consider either investigation as coming within normal police procedure.

He was intrigued to know, from his quick but thorough boning up on the present case, that it again brought him in contact with the young woman antique dealer with the parson husband. He had quite fancied her, with her slim waist and big eyes and soft voice, and looked forward to putting her through it again – more successfully this time, he hoped. She had a kid now, he gathered, and was still married to that peculiar parson. He wondered if the Welsh sidekick of hers, the dealer, was still on pot, or worse, and could be got at in some way.

All this was relish to the crime itself. He'd read the press reports, which to him made too much of the thing. He had plenty of experience in Forensic, and had told numerous unmoved pathologists about an early case of his involving a corpse which had been cut up into pieces and hidden in a lodging house in all sorts of surprising places. Mere decapitation was peanuts, to that. His favourite classic crime was the 1920s Crumbles murder at Eastbourne.

The people he questioned at Elvesham's Murder Incident Room were just what he would have chosen. He insisted on seeing them again, in spite of having their statements already. The husband first, of course, in the usual state of distress. If these widowers only knew how lucky they were, getting rid of their wives in one blow (very apt, that, in this case) instead of putting up with years of nagging as he, Ogle, had, before his divorce.

Euan French was accompanied by Rodney Chelmarsh, there to give him moral strength. Rodney's unconsciously appropriate quotation as they entered had really been said to himself alone, but, unfortunately, aloud. Poor Euan was not at all morally strengthened to hear *The prisoner comes to meet his doom, The block, the headsman, and the tomb.* The wild look he threw at Ogle was meat and drink to the detective.

But, bait and snap as he would, there was no admission to be got out of the man that he had quarrelled with his wife before her disappearance or that he knew of any reason why she should have been murdered. He merely repeated his statements and stuck fast by them.

As Ogle reluctantly let him go, Euan asked nervously, 'When will . . . they let me bury her?'

Ogle laughed. It seemed to him a genuinely funny question.

'Not much hope of that. Not till Forensic's taken a good look and got itself together about the time of death. Could be weeks, depending what they've got on.'

'You must have a lot to get through this morning,' Rodney said hastily, and as hastily he removed his charge, leaving Ogle wishing he had some excuse for grilling the parson.

'I just want,' Euan stammered, 'I want her to be decently laid to rest. Covered up. You know. Not like that.'

'Of course. Don't worry,' Rodney murmured. *When she in well-earned grave Within the hour is duly laid . . .*

Max Johnston's statement was a delight to Ogle, who goaded him into becoming violently abusive. Ogle dictated to his sergeant loudly, clearly, that he considered Mr Johnston potentially violent, and that he should be kept under surveillance.

Max drew a huge, deep breath, as he had been trained to do, and slowly let it out again. He said no more. Later that morning he and Amy checked out of the Rose and returned on the noon train to London.

Rupert Wylie had not turned up. His office thought he was showing a house to a prospective buyer somewhere on the other side of Abbotsbourne. Ogle swore. 'Can't go chasing after him now. Mrs Chelmarsh.'

He had deliberately kept her waiting. She was angry, and not prepared to be toyed with.

'Ah, Miss . . . no, Mrs, isn't it? And how's the antiques business doing?'

She was talking to a pike, she told herself firmly, a stuffed pike that had been programmed to open its jaws and snap. Well, let it try.

'Not particularly good. It may get even worse if I don't reach the sale I'm going to on time. I've nothing to add to my statement, if that's what you were going to ask me. I know nothing about Mrs French's life that would be likely to provoke anyone into murdering her. Nobody in Elvesham or Abbotsbourne had the faintest motive for it, to my knowledge. Anything else?'

Ogle surveyed her with disappointment. Yes, she had got prettier, more rounded, a bit fuller round both areas. Pale, though, for summer, looked as if she hadn't been sleeping a lot.

'Nasty shock for you, finding the body, was it? Didn't expect a hacked-around corpse in one of your nice old antiques?'

Doran met his mocking eyes unflinchingly, though he had deliberately conjured up a sight she was trying very hard to blot out.

'No, naturally I didn't. And it wasn't my antique, as you suggest, it was hired from a dealer in Eastgate, a Mr Wedderbell. I believe he wasn't to be found when the police searched his premises.' She had no intention of mentioning that she had been present. 'I should advise you to follow him up. Is there anything else you want to ask me?'

Ogle was annoyed to find that there was not. He let her go, frowning after her.

What a Shadbolt he'd have made, she reflected, running to her car. *The nice regulation of a thumbscrew* would have suited him to perfection. I bet that's what they were like, the people who worked racks and iron maidens and all the other horrors. They really liked assistant tormenting.

Back at the Incident Room, Ogle was irritated to find that the rest of his cast were not prepared to uproot themselves from whatever they were doing and come to him. Hugo Snaresby, Ralph Chapman and Alex Warner, all in their respective offices, replied politely that they had already made a statement and had nothing to add. Rupert Wylie, who had reappeared, replied impolitely that he wasn't bloody going to waste another minute on inquiries which the police ought to be following up themselves, and anyway he had to take his wife to hospital for a check-up.

Only Jack Turner presented himself, reluctantly, because he disliked what the sight of a police car outside his shop might do for trade. Sullenly he repeated his regrets for having sharpened the chopper.

Ogle put on his grimmest face.

'Well, if they find the blow was administered by a professional, we shall know where to look, that's all. Do something stupid, take the consequences. Eh?'

He was looking forward to questioning another woman. Another Doran type, possibly? Or something a bit riper. Maggie Culffe.

But Maggie was sitting at her brother's bedside in Barminster's large modern hospital. Guided by an immaculately made-up white-coated girl looking like a *Vogue* model seen through a soft lens, Ogle found Maggie by way of endless gleaming slippery corridors.

Oh, disappointment. Late thirties, too fat, wrong sort of spectacles, drinks. Hardly worth being alone in a cubicle with except for a WPC, but duty was duty.

It was obvious that she had not come to the hospital unarmed. Gin was all around her, like a cloud of room-freshener or fly-spray. But she was strong in the head, a tigress in defence of her cub, prepared to hold back her roars for his sake.

'My brother's a very sensitive boy. He's been delicate all his life.'

Ogle looked pointedly from the face on the pillow to hers.

'Big family, is it? Him at one end of the line, you at the other?'

Maggie set her mouth. She was not going to take offence that might prove dangerous.

'He's only my half-brother, but I've always felt for him as if . . . there's no difference.'

She stroked the boy's damp hair tenderly, her hand hovering as though she would have liked to pull up the sheet to cover his naked shoulders.

Remorselessly Ogle put her through it: Guy's relations with women, his particular relations with Mrs French. How many times had they met?

'Not many – that I know of.'

'Could be others you don't know of?'

Maggie shrugged. 'I doubt it. I know pretty well where he is.'

'Your brother's keeper, eh? But you did know how he felt about her.'

'I knew he found her attractive, of course, anyone could see that. Guy's got a very affectionate nature, and she'd been kind to him when – when someone else wasn't. I'm sure it hadn't gone any further.'

'He'd had girlfriends before, of course.'

'I wouldn't call Mrs French a girlfriend.'

'Had he or hadn't he?' Ogle barked. 'Or was he some kind of poof?'

Maggie's flush darkened. 'You've no right . . .' She collected herself. Lines from *Yeomen* twisted themselves and teased her. *With sisterly readiness, for my fair brother's sake . . .*

'Of course he'd had girlfriends,' she said, and Ogle noted her clenched knuckles, her eyes turned away from his.

'Ever known him get violent with them? Love-bites, rough stuff, physical damage of any kind?'

The WPC moved forward swiftly as Maggie's tears suddenly spilt over.

'No,' she sobbed, 'no, no no! He wouldn't hurt a fly. God knows I've had the care of him since – since he lost his mother. Leave me alone, oh do leave me alone.'

Ogle, uncharacteristically, did.

The door shut. Through the glass top half of it Maggie unnoticingly saw white-coated forms flit past. Now the pressure was off, she need no longer talk about poor Guy. They could have roused him, broken the sound barrier that kept him still and lifeless-looking on that narrow bed. He hadn't heard them, though, that hateful policeman and her. Perhaps he would never hear anything again. Perhaps the needle on that screen would waver, and stop, and the drip-feed no longer nourish his drained-out body.

She took a pull from the half-bottle of gin in her shoulder-bag, and sat, as motionless as Guy, contemplating her guilt.

The girl. Five years ago. After Guy had lost his mother, and gone a bit wild – not wicked, just wild. They had suspected him of all sorts of local misdeeds, a warehouse fire, the theft of video equipment, smashed windows . . . He owned up to some of them.

Then, the worst thing. A headline: Body of girl found in garden shed. Schoolboy helping police with their inquiries. The girl had died after a 'chasing the dragon' session with other teenagers in the garden shed of an empty house. The autopsy had shown bruises on her throat, and Guy's name was brought up. Hadn't he been her boyfriend?

He'd denied it. There had been some sort of struggle, he said. 'She wouldn't let me. I don't remember any more.'

Maggie had undertaken to act as his guardian, and he had been given a stern warning.

But never the same again, poor Guy. Somehow she, Maggie, had failed him.

12

A story grim and gory

It seemed months rather than days that Euan had been at Bell House.

Not that he behaved obtrusively. He was quiet, self-effacing, considerate. Doran would have given him a four-star award as a boarder. He insisted on handing her a wad of notes to cover heating, lighting and food, of which he consumed very little. He paid scrupulously for every telephone call he made, most of them to his mother-in-law in Stafford, who seemed incapable of understanding what had happened or of making an actual appearance. His frantic talks with her on the telephone every evening were very difficult not to overhear.

'We could ask him to use the bedroom extension,' Doran suggested desperately after three discreet abandonings of their drawing room to his silent plea for the use of the instrument.

'No.' Rodney's tone admitted of no argument.

The trouble with Euan was that he was there. The days were free, when he was at work, once their morning use of the bathroom had been deflected to the little cloakroom off the old hallway, and their breakfast conversation had been inhibited by Euan's almost silent, infinitely depressing presence.

In the evenings it was impossible to enjoy TV with him in the room, staring unseeingly at the screen, or to read without being conscious of him, or simply to sit about and chat after Kit had been put to bed.

'I feel so guilty!' Doran burst out on the fourth evening, when he was safely out of the house, on one of the rare visits to his own home which she knew he found unbearably painful. 'Knowing he's envying us, as he said. Being complacent about ourselves and Kit. Even wondering if in some way I was responsible for – what happened.'

Or whether you were, she silently added. There had been that night when the key of the Old Primary School had been added to the huge prop ring which was to be hooked in Shadbolt's belt. Rodney had left it in the keyhole all night, an invitation for someone unauthorized to let themselves in.

Suddenly she was unsure of that or anything else to do with the horrible case. Impossible to shift the burden to Rodney; he had enough to bear. And surely – on a wave of relief, she remembered Max saying he'd found the key sticking in the lock after Rodney had left. She could tell him that and lighten his conscience.

But she must talk to someone else.

Lydia Eastry was hanging out washing in the garden of the house in the pleasant, ordinary seaside suburb. It was bigger than the police house at Abbotsbourne, the garden twice the size, giving scope for one of Sam's special hobbies. Now it was a blaze of flowers. The grass was immaculately cut, as though at a county cricket ground.

Lydia turned her pretty head, grey by now in her middle age, at the click of the gate.

'Doran! what a surprise. Nice one, I mean.' She made a swift neat fold-up of the washing yet unhung and came forward. Comely, kindly, with a touch of Northern bluntness in her manner – Sam had been lucky in his wife. Their daughter Jennifer, absorbed in whatever she was playing at in a sand-pit, looked up and gave Doran a cheerful grin. A few months older than Kit, she was a big-boned sturdy child very like her mother.

Lydia and Doran chatted about Abbotsbourne news before Doran came to the point of her visit.

'Is he in? They said at the nick that he was off duty.'

'He is – down at the back, in the vegetable patch. He'll be glad to see you.'

Sam's pleasure was mingled with anxiety. He knew Doran and her propensity for getting dangerously mixed up in things.

But he greeted her warmly, showed her some new knobbly vegetables which looked as though they'd be an awful nuisance to peel, and offered her a sawn-off tree stump to sit on.

'This is a social visit, is it?' he asked hopefully.

'That question is put expecting the answer No, as in Latin grammar, isn't it, Sam?'

'If you say so, Doran. Somehow I didn't think it was just the pleasure of my company.'

'Oh, but that's part of it. I do like this house, and seeing Lydia and Jennifer again – what a jolly girl she is. But actually I wanted to talk to you about the Elvesham business. I feel I haven't helped you about it. I've been – thinking about something else. Why didn't I do more – follow things up.'

Sam regarded her benevolently.

'Because there was no need to. It wasn't your place. You don't have to find the murderer. You didn't even like Mrs French, did you? Why not just lay off it?'

'Because it was such an ugly murder. And so – oh, what's the right word – incongruous. Mixed up with innocent things, like *Yeomen*, and . . .' Tiggy's beautiful face swam into her mind, changing what she had been going to say.

'Murder's always ugly,' Sam said.

'Yes, of course. But Paula was so young. *Death whene'er he call, must call too soon.* He called much too soon for her, poor creature. Where *was* she killed? Obviously not where I found her. I should have asked you before – why didn't I? Do they know?'

'Oh, they know. In the school garden. Somebody had piled broken branches and dead leaves and rubbish over the grass. It wasn't difficult to find.'

Doran shivered. 'I remember. Wild lavender and a sort of late-autumn smell. And a lot of insects, too many. I remember thinking it was a nasty garden, not the sort you'd choose for a production of *As You Like It*, for instance. I feel terrible about it all now, Sam, almost as though I'd wished her dead, being so spiteful. And there's poor Euan, absolutely broken up – they might as well have killed him too. I wish I liked him better. I don't, you know, and that doesn't make me feel good. Well, I shall go on trying, though I know you don't approve.'

Sam shook his head. He was glad to be shut of this case, and wished Doran wouldn't mix herself up in it. But he had known she would, now that the emotional thing had passed. He watched her, at the garden gate, greet a tall youth with a near-punk haircut and one gold earring. He slouched unbecomingly. He was Ben, Sam's son, going through the phase all parents dread. Jennifer would be the same, when the time came. But not yet, thank Heaven – she was still his baby. He gave the peculiar whistle that was her signal. She clambered out of her sand-pit and came running to him, clasping his knees and looking up with adoring admiration at him, her Daddy, her God.

Doran drove back to her shop, restless and dissatisfied. Howell was unpacking items from a large box and appraising them.

'Somebody brought some smalls?' she asked, though it was obvious that someone had.

'Brighouse. Picked them up yesterday and thought of you. Staffs flatbacks, couple of Fairyland plates, little walnut teapoy, eighteen ten-ish – nice, isn't it? Oh, and a couple of stumpwork pics, but I made him take 'em back.'

'You *what?* You know I passionately love stumpwork.'

'Oh, you wouldn't have loved these, gel – badly faded, been in strong light, one of 'em had moth. Dull subjects, too, Old Testament guys dressed up in Charles Two frills. No, we'd hardly have got a turn on 'em.'

To his appalled astonishment Doran's eyes filled with angry tears.

'I wouldn't have offered them. They were for *me*. I'd have kept them at home, they'd have been something fresh to look at and find out about. Oh, how could you be so stupid?' She sat down suddenly and gave way to tears, Howell staring at her in consternation.

'What's the matter with you, then? You're not in pod again, are you?'

'Hywel.' His mother appeared from the back room. 'Don't go on at her. What do you know about ladies in pod? Anyway – she isn't, I can always tell. You come in here with me, Doran. Sit there, it's a terrible hard chair but I've brought a cushion for it. Now, I can see you're upset, and anybody else would say they'd just put the kettle on and how about a nice cup of tea. Well, I've got a better idea.'

She opened the cupboard where Howell kept supplies, and produced a half bottle of champagne.

'Better for you than tea. Lifts the spirits. Takes the weight.' She opened the bottle expertly, swiftly, a thing Doran had never seen a woman do and very few men. She poured, into two very pretty 1760-ish glasses which Doran recognized as being from stock.

'*Iechyd da.*' She drank. Doran followed her, surprisingly calmed by the first draught of the wine and by the hypnotic glitter of Gwenllian's purple sweater, on which cavorted a white swan with diamanté eyes, hung about with gold chains, its stitchcrafted feathers dotted here and there with sparkles of silver, waterdrops of sequin.

'. . . only High Street champagne, of course,' Gwenllian was saying, 'but makes no difference, does you a world of good. You listen to me, *merch.* I can see things, you know, the way your friend Amy thought she could but she couldn't. I can see you in the middle of a black cloud, very nasty, very evil. Thoughts and feelings and deeds, all evil. Some of it in you, in your heart. Understand?'

'Yes. Very well.' Doran's tears had stopped.

'So, get rid of it, of the poison. You know how.'

Doran did. She must confront the thing, exorcize it, forget it.

'This murder, now that's outside you, but it's drawing you in, sending out a black web to catch you. You like ghost stories, now, I would bet on that. But you wouldn't care at all to have an elemental crawling about your house, showing itself in all sorts of filthy nasty scaring shapes. It could make for you, or Rodney, or your little boy, and then what would happen? I know about these things, you see, I'm an Old Soul. If you don't take care, the *ellyau* will have you and yours.' She nodded several times, emphatically. 'Keep out of it. Go home. You've got a son, I've got a son. I didn't bring mine up quite right, not all my fault, and he went a bit off the straight. You want to be around when yours is growing up, don't you?'

'Yes. Oh, yes.'

'You heed me, then. I won't say anything more of this, I don't do it that often.' Gwenllian finished her drink, and as she did so instantly was transformed from a sybil with secret, dark knowledge, to a chirpy little elderly woman.

'What's happening to your Kit, then, since your glamorous friend left?'

'Well, Rodney's looking after him, and Vi, that's my lady help, comes in when she can. He was fairly upset over – Tiggy – going, and he isn't really himself, poor little boy. But we manage.'

'Not good enough, managing. I'll go up there and look after him. If you agree.' Gwenllian's manner was almost shy.

Doran didn't answer at once. There was certainly a need for someone to look after Kit if she was to be free to work, and Rodney to carry out his parish duties and radio commitments. Vi worked for other families, she was not free to take over.

But did Doran want someone who had brought up the boy who had become Howell to be in charge of her son? And could this startling, dynamic stranger, almost a foreigner, be trusted? What would be her effect on Rodney, on Vi (herself highly critical), most of all on Kit himself, who had not met Gwenllian? She hesitated. Gwenllian spoke for her.

'Look in my eyes.'

They were dark and bright, and shone with something Doran recognized. The power for good, the strength of virtue. She had seen it in Rodney's.

'All right. Yes. Thank you very much indeed,' she said, feeling inadequate.

'It won't be for long, mind, just the rest of the summer. Hywel will like having the place to himself again. Now, Kit. He enjoys a story?'

'Loves them.'

'I have a lot of them.' She ticked them off on her fingers. 'I shall tell him tales from the Mabinogion and all about the wars of Owain Glyn Dŵr, who was a great magician, you know, and Twm Sion Catti, the Robin Hood of Cymru. And the *twlywth teg*, though I must watch how much I say about *them*. And I can look after children well and cook very nice too.'

'You're a miracle. I don't deserve you but I'll take you, gladly.'

'And no more going into the black cloud.'

'No more.' Except for one thing . . .

Peg was at his favourite spot, painting. Some boats were moored nearby, which he was lovingly setting against a sea of dark pearl. Doran sat down on the sand beside him.

'I want to find Ken Wedderbell, Peg.'

'You'll be lucky. The police haven't. I hear things, you know, and from what I hear they've tried everywhere – all the departments at the Town Hall, Social Security, Health, Sheltered Accommodation, even the Samaritans. They're not allowed to give names, but they'd tell if they *hadn't* heard from him. Why are you so keen to find Ken?'

'Well. Ostensibly I want to tell him about what happened to his coffer, and what he'd like done about it, in the way of cleaning. And I want to know who's going to be at his shop, if you can call it one, to take in the props I borrowed and hand over a receipt for them. That woman upstairs obviously isn't going to make herself responsible. And . . .

'Something else – I want to find out where he got all that furniture, and what's the matter with him, and why he isn't a kosher dealer. Just to put the record straight. Other dealers do have a right to know, don't they?'

'Oh, sure.' Peg swiftly painted a flash of white, a seagull in flight. 'Could be he'd release some into the trade, if you asked him nicely.'

'What a cynic you are. Can you see anyone selling that grotesque coffer, after its recent history?'

'Yes. With a load of hoo-hah and publicity, for a nice fat price.'

'Oh.' Doran thought of Gwenllian's black cloud of evil, the cloud she would be pulling other people into if any action of hers led to the carved chest being sold on. And the *ellyau*, whatever they were. A private buyer might be landed with the chest, or Madame Tussaud's Chamber of Horrors, but wherever it went it would do no good.

'So. Where do I find Wedderbell?'

An angry – or shifty – look, and some rapid brush-work on the sky area. 'I just told you.'

'No, you told me where I couldn't find him. I'd like to know where you first heard all this stuff you told me about him, nicking things from a stately home or museum or something.' Yes, definitely shifty, but at last, his small mouth sulky, he told her:

'Beachcombers.'

Eastgate had the normal seaside quota of layabouts, junkies, teenage rebels, collectors of scrap, bag-ladies and their like who spent a lot of their unimaginably dull lives under the old pier, where it joined the sea wall that protected the promenade. It was news to Doran that Peg had anything to do with these sad creatures. Hard to imagine him visiting them for charitable reasons, taking them, as it were, hot dinners, nourishing soup, Gideon Bibles.

No. There was something odd, farouche, about Peg, apart from his nautical get-up and unfathomable relationship with his wife. Something that tied up with the beach-folk and their ways, what they drank, or smoked, or talked about.

But this was not the time to explore it.

'Thanks. I'll have a slight wander – I might just see him.' She got up. 'And do thank Meg very much for taking on herself to return all the costumes – it's saved me so much trouble. Oh – and the one she made for

Rodney, I think he might like to keep, as a souvenir. Okay?'

Peg sketched a sort of salute, his eyes on his painting. He was sorry he had told her, and he would like her to leave as soon as possible.

The day was sultry, an afternoon of low-hanging clouds reflecting like steel on the quiet sea. A lot of holidaymakers were still about, swimming or sitting in deckchairs, wearing beach-wraps or almost nothing. Old people strolled on the marina above, slow, arm in arm. Children and dogs splashed, screamed and barked, parents threw bright striped balls to them. The seaside resorts of England were unchanged in essence, just very sparsely populated since the throngs of sea-and-sun-starved townies had taken to the Costas.

A naked toddler ran shrieking from its mother and fell almost at Doran's feet. She picked it up and consoled it, thinking with a pang of Kit and how much she wished he were with her, on an innocent, ordinary excursion. But this was something else.

She almost missed seeing Wedderbell, prone in the dark shadow of the pier. He could have been a corpse, but for the irregular stertorous snoring. There was no one near him. A hundred yards or so away a boy and girl lay in such a close embrace it was impossible to see where either began or ended, prone and motionless.

Doran approached the unconscious man and shook his shoulder. An empty gin bottle lay beside him, under his lax hand. He made no sign of having felt her touch. She repeated the shake, saying his name loudly.

Now the eyelids flickered, and the bleary eyes opened in the empurpled, pimply face, thick in white stubble. This must have been how Dickens intended Newman Noggs at his worst to look, but was too fond of the character to say so. How obtuse of Ogle and his men not to have traced Wedderbell here – even among drifters, he was easy enough to spot without bothering the Town Hall.

At last he came back from a very far distance. Comprehension returned to his eyes. Was it imagination that there was recognition in them?

'Mr Wedderbell,' she said, 'it's me, Doran Fairweather.' That was how Peg had introduced her. 'I'm a dealer. I've got a shop in Quay Street. I'm glad I've found you. Do you remember me?'

He slowly sat up, propping himself against the wet-gleaming wall, staring at her.

'Yes,' he answered, his voice slow and thick. The voice of a ruin, but a gentlemanly ruin. 'You came . . . somebody brought you. Furniture. For the theatre.'

'Not exactly that, the amateur stage, a production of *The Yeomen of the Guard.* I hired two joint-stools, a spinning wheel and – a coffer, a carved chest. You said it had been made specially for stage use. Remember?'

His right hand closed on the gin bottle. Slowly, awesomely, he said, '*Has thou found me out, O mine enemy?*'

The boy and girl were still the only people in sight, still in their clenched embrace, unmoving. It was said that when you wanted a policeman there was never one in sight – Doran would have given a lot for the sudden appearance even of Ogle. Wedderbell's hand was thin, but strong enough to . . . strong enough. The long, grimy fingers were gripping the bottle-neck tightly and a broken bottle can make an awful mess of one's face.

Doran backed away. He would have to get to his feet to reach her.

'I'm not your enemy,' she said, in the loud clear tones of an infant-school teacher. 'I'm just a dealer, and I don't know anything about you. I came to tell you that we haven't used your furniture at all, and I want to know if you could tell me what would be a good time to return it, when there'd be somebody to take it in, you know.'

He said nothing, but the hand still held the bottle.

'And I wanted to break it to you that something really horrifying happened, to do with the chest. I don't know how to begin to explain.'

His left hand came up to cover his face, and he made a sound between a cry and a groan.

'A – a body got into it, you see . . .'

She could see the eyes now, wild like a frightened horse's, red-seamed.

'A woman was killed – murdered – somewhere else, and then whoever did it got into the building where our stage was and hid the body. I'm afraid it was a very messy, nasty murder, and it made a bit of a mess of the chest. Would you like to have it professionally cleaned for you, by a restorer? When the police have finished with it, that is.'

'A woman,' he said. 'It was a woman this time.'

'This time?'

'Yes. Last time it was a man, you see. Ralph. My – my dear friend. The boy – the victim, oh my God – in *Rope*. I was in the theatre then, you see. Oh, not an actor, except for walk-ons. Just a dogsbody, a stagehand.'

I'm not really hearing this, Doran thought, it's something to do with the acoustics under the pier. *Rope*, he had mentioned that the coffer had been used in the old thriller by Patrick Hamilton, about the two wicked young men who kill another, just for kicks, and hide the body in a chest.

'Yes, how interesting,' she put in mildly. 'Do go on.'

'Ralph was a pro, he'd made it, while I was still heaving flats about. And shifting furniture.'

Doran made sympathetic noises.

'I knew he was mixing with – those others. I knew

he'd gone over to them, I'd lose him.' He glared suddenly. 'Why am I telling you all this?'

'Because it's so important that I ought to know it.'

'He left my flat and went to share with David. I was so jealous, so very, bitterly jealous.' Tears rolled down the raddled cheeks. 'So I stopped up the holes in the chest. The ventilation holes that had been drilled.'

A wave of chill struck Doran.

'He was in there for most of an act – I think. With all the party music going on they couldn't hear him. But I could.' A long shudder shook him. 'He must have – given up – quite early. When they lifted the lid he was dead. Of course.'

Doran moved further away.

'What happened?' she asked. 'Did they find out?'

'They found the plugged holes, yes. But I gave myself up, because I was so sorry. Ralph, poor Ralph. I don't remember much after that, but they put me in a terrible place with mad people. I think I must have been there for a long time, because my hair used to be brown, and when they let me out it was like this. They told me I'd missed a war. I suppose I was lucky, in a way.' He fingered his wispy scalp, smiling vaguely.

Doran felt strongly that she would rather not know any more of this dreadful story. It was clear to her that the version Peg had given her – nervous breakdown, asylum confinement, conscience – had been garbled to fit the earlier crime, not the stealing of museum exhibits.

There was only one thing more to ask.

'Why did you go to Elvesham?'

He looked blank.

'The village where we were putting on the opera. I saw you, remember, in a thunderstorm, outside the school building.'

'Oh.' A crazed brain trying to remember. 'I found out where it was. Someone knew. I think the men who came for it told me. I had to see it again, so I went on the bus.'

'It' must be the chest. Murderer returns to scene of crime.

'I saw it,' he said, quite sanely. 'I saw her lying there, in the garden, all blood. It was night by then. I didn't want to see it any more. I was frightened. So I went home.'

From the back pocket of his trousers, which she noticed were old-fashioned and had once been part of a suit, not the statutory jeans of Eastgate, he produced another half bottle with a three-star label, and drank thirstily from it. Doran murmured polite thanks, and faded away.

An imperturbable sergeant at Eastgate nick took down her story as calmly as though she were reporting the whereabouts of a missing cat, and promised to relay the whole to Chief Inspector Ogle, when he returned to the station.

'Tell him Wedderbell's quite unbalanced,' she added. 'Seems harmless, but I'm not entirely convinced he is. He wants remedial treatment soon, before he does any harm to himself or anybody else. I thought you'd better know where he is. He's had a terrible shock. That's all.'

A morbid desire seized her to examine the chest again for the ventilation holes. She dismissed it as nasty and unworthy. And of course the thing was now in police custody.

From the shop she rang Barminster Hospital to inquire about Guy Culffe's condition. The reply was 'very poorly' – practically a knell, in hospital phraseology.

'Why don't you go home?' Howell emerged from the depths of a longcase he was dissecting. 'No, I didn't listen to what Mam was sayin' to you, rabbitin' on, because she thinks women have got their own talk and no one else has a dictionary. But I can tell you these opera folk don't want you, and the Bill don't want you, I don't want you, and Rod and Kit do. Mam's with 'em now, but she's not you, is she? Go on home.'

'Thanks, Howell. I will.'

13

Yet one would pray to live

Rodney's gaze strayed wistfully towards the television papers, wandering over programme billings. He longed to be able to switch on the set and sit back with it, accepting the anodyne of familiar entertainment. Cricket highlights tonight, from a match he'd missed during the day, and the start of a new drama series.

Doran and he knew exactly what the other liked or did not like to watch. They had the video perfectly in control between them, this for his leisure time, that for hers, junior programmes, very carefully sifted, for Kit's amusement or edification at a chosen time of day. It all worked beautifully.

Except for Euan. During what seemed to have been a stay comparable to the Victorian custom of landing oneself on distant relatives for anything from three to six months, they had discovered nothing that he enjoyed watching. He would stare at the screen glumly, showing no glimmer of interest, silently defying anyone else to enjoy whatever was on it. Except that scenes of violence, especially physical attack, would make him jump and cry out.

It seemed callous to inflict comedy on him. Archaeology and history clearly bored him, and programmes which might remind him of Paula's many skills were so frequent that Doran had taken to checking the programmes every morning for features on fashions or cookery which she would have watched herself.

Until, one morning when the evening promised no less than three such programmes, and she re-folded the paper. It was no use. The Spectre at the Feast was with them, until they could persuade him to move somewhere, anywhere.

But this evening, tired after a long and wearing day of radio interviews with garrulous or querulous old people, Rodney forgot the house rule.

'*A Corpse for the Coroner*,' he read out. 'Telecrime getting more and more realistic. In the good old days you'd never have heard a whisper about what one might call the seamy side of death at all – just a glimpse of a shrouded form or the back of someone's head . . .'

'Rodney,' Doran said.

'But now, it's absolutely otherwise. The full horrors, including obligatory scene of mortuary slab with forensic details. I do wonder – '

Euan put his hand to his mouth and ran from the room, retching and choking. Doran shook her head at Rodney.

'How could you?'

'I know, I know, don't tell me. I'm a brutal wretch, I'm a model of tactlessness. I'm a disgrace to the cloth. Nobody could blame me more than I do. I begin to wonder if I've taken so many funeral services that I've become immune. Do you think it's that?'

'No, of course not. You just forgot for a minute. Damn it, there's nothing one *can* say to the man! I've even – I hate to admit this, but I've even stopped being sorry for him.'

They looked at each other silently. Both needed, for different reasons, a time of domestic peace, Rodney to exorcize his memory of Tiggy and his own great offence against Doran, she to make peace with her past doubts and fears. After that wound to their marriage, there must be a healing normality. Instead they were disrupted by this gloomy, preoccupied stranger, who gave off an almost visible black ray of depression.

'I can feel it getting into the curtains,' Doran said.

'I'd like to have the whole house renewed, wallpaper and paint and all, like that American millionairess, the one who has it done every three months. No, I wouldn't really, because there are too many things I'm fond of. But what's the good? He just won't go.'

'I think we give him security, of a sort. A sense of family.'

'If he wants family why doesn't he get that mother-in-law of his to come down from the Potteries or wherever and keep house for him?'

'You know as much as I do. Perhaps she'll stay after the funeral.'

'When there *is* a funeral,' Doran said. 'The police won't release – Paula until they know who did it. And they're no nearer.'

Gwenllian materialized at the door. It was the only description for her way of appearing quietly, without creeping up on one. So small she was and so light-footed, it was, Doran thought, like having a fairy godmother in the house. After all, Cinderella would need some calm restorative influence after all that chaos with the glass slipper and finding herself a princess instead of a chimney-corner drudge. A puff of smoke, a waft of perfume, and behold! the person who can make pumpkins into coaches and rats into spanking steeds.

Gwenllian, so much needed.

She kept herself to herself, without appearing in the least reclusive or stand-offish. A small room in the old part of the house, one of those that had been Helena's, she had made into what she obviously regarded as her sanctum and headquarters. Doran, without ever having entered it, knew that it was scrupulously kept and always had flowers in it.

Over Kit, Gwenllian exercised a strong fascination. Under her influence he forgot Tiggy in a matter of days. 'Gwen' had a voice like strange music, on whose rhythms he was borne up and down, listening intently to her tales, some of them highly unsuitable but all spellbinding. While she talked, or sang her songs about skipping lambs and Dewi Sant and Sweet Jenny Jones, he liked to play with the silver charms on her bracelet, or the chains and beads that clustered round her neck, hiding what age had done to it. She was light and silence and peace and wisdom to him, and Doran had been ashamed to feel a distinct pang of jealousy. Of course, it wasn't the same when a person was only in charge of one's child for a limited period, but . . . Perhaps new mothers had a lot to learn.

'Was your little boy like me?' she heard Kit asking Gwenllian.

'Not much, love, no. But you know him, don't you, your Uncle Hywel.'

Kit stared at her. 'He's not your little boy. He's a man, like Daddy.'

'Well, he was. We all change – just like Queen Rhiannon's son in my story.'

'Oh.' The cat Tybalt came towards them, inviting notice and Kit's attention wandered. 'How about Twm Sion Catti again.'

'Well. That was not his real name, you understand, but he looked so much like a handsome young black tomcat that the Welsh folk called him that. He could ride like the wind . . .'

Ozzy, Doran's half-gypsy gardener, was engaged in his favourite occupation of leaning on a spade. He was listening to Gwenllian's story with something like childish awe. Doran had noticed that his manner to Gwenllian was more respectful than the one he used to the family, and free of expletives. He had, also, never stolen anything connected with her. Once before, in the case of the Carved Cherub, Ozzy had shown signs of what Rodney diagnosed as Britano-Roman beliefs with Christian overtones.

'You don't talk to Gwenllian a lot yourself,' she commented to Rodney. 'Don't you like her?'

'I admire her immensely. She knows a lot more than I do, and I find that most impressive. And she's marvellous with Kit.'

'But there's something, isn't there?'

Rodney smiled. 'Yes, my darling. We practise different forms of magic, and I don't think it would do for either of us to evangelize.'

'Ah. In other words, you wouldn't set up a Mithraic altar in St Leonard's, however nice a piece of stone it was?'

'Exactly. No.' How splendid, Rodney thought, that he would never need to tell anyone that his wife didn't understand him.

Doran sighed. 'Mithraic or Celtic or whatever, I wish she'd wave a wand to get rid of Euan. But as she never seems to speak to him except very politely at meals, I really don't know her attitude to him. I *could* just ask her . . .'

And when she did, Gwenllian answered directly, dispassionately.

'Oh, I've little to say to him or he to me. I know you find him an intruder here, but he'll go when he has to. As I will.'

An evening came when Euan entered the dining room with a different look on his face from its usual glumness. He was set to tell them something, Doran felt. As they sat down to her starter of grilled grapefruit, out it came abruptly.

'Doran. Rodney. I might as well tell you now. I'm going.'

Two pairs of joyful, still unbelieving eyes met his.

'Oh, where?' Rodney asked with deceptive calm. 'Back next door?'

'No, I couldn't. I'm selling it. I've got a transfer.'

'That's nice for you. Nearer to Paula's mother?' Doran tried to keep rapture out of her voice.

'No. A place in Tyne and Wear. I'm starting next week. So I'm going next door to pack up my personal stuff tonight, and a moving firm will come and do the furniture later on. I'll stay on till tomorrow, if that's all right with you, and then I'm going up there to find a flat.'

His hosts could hardly eat their meal for happy excitement. When he had excused himself and left before the coffee, as he usually did, they turned eagerly to each other.

'Can it be true?' Doran cried. 'Can it really be true, or a lovely dream?'

Rodney burst into song.

'*Oh, Sergeant Meryll, is it true –*
The welcome news we read in orders?'

Doran said, 'Not really a case, though, of *I have been kindly tended, and I almost fear I am loth to go?* Not a word of gratitude, the swine, for all the feeding and washing and cleaning I've done for that man, and the inconvenience, and the gloom. Not a word!'

Rodney, now loudly euphoric, carolled,

'*With an ounce or two of lead*
I dispatched him through the head!'

'No, we didn't even have to do that – what a pity. By the way, did you know (this is from my G. and S. Mishaps collection) that one Phoebe got muddled when telling Shadbolt in the last scene about Fairfax – *whom thou has just shot through the bottom, and who lies at the head of the river.* Instead of the other way round, of course.'

They collapsed into laughter among the remains of the meal. Doran was the first to recover herself.

'We must calm down, or he'll hear us. He – '

An emphatic, unreal cough interrupted her. Euan stood in the doorway.

'I meant to tell you before, I've put my house on

the market. So you may be getting callers and phone inquiries, as from tomorrow.'

'Thanks,' Doran said, now serious again, 'but I'm afraid neither of us will be in. It won't be really convenient.'

'Oh. Well, that's a nuisance. I don't want to have to give Dixter and Wylie a key.'

'They're a perfectly reliable firm. I'm sure they can be trusted.'

'Maybe. I don't like that young bastard, though, Rupert. They can send somebody else.'

'I expect they'll send one of their girls,' Doran said coldly. 'There's no particular reason why it should be their junior partner. Perhaps you'd prefer old Mr Dixter?' she added with sarcasm. Henry Dixter was eighty and visited the office not more than once or twice a week.

'Yes, I would.' Euan threw her a cold stare, and left them.

'Oh dear.' Rodney shut the door after him. 'I'm afraid he heard us. Embarrassing.'

'What can he do? In any case, only tonight, and that's it.'

'Oh joy, oh rapture unforeseen,
For now the sky is all serene – '

Rodney had switched operas and forgotten discretion. There was a tap at the door: they both jumped guiltily.

The person who had tapped came into the room. Maggie Culffe was quite sober, for once, and thinner than she had been. There were traces of tears on her cheeks.

'I'm sorry to butt in,' she said. 'You sounded so cheerful, I thought it might be a party.'

'It is, in a way. Sit down, Maggie. Is there any coffee left in the pot, Rod? What news of Guy? I did ring the hospital yesterday but the person who answered was very cagey. Oh. You haven't come to say . . .'

Maggie sank into a chair and put her head back in collapse, her eyes shut. Doran checked that a brandy bottle was available on a side table.

'He's better,' Maggie said at last. 'He's out of the coma. They're sure he'll be all right now. Yesterday they didn't want to say too much.'

'Thank God,' said Rodney.

'Yes, thank God. I can hardly believe it. My poor Guy. I'm still so thankful it wasn't me that killed him.'

'Killed him?' Rodney spoke very quietly.

'Yes. I thought I had done. I gave him an overdose, you see, a lot more than he usually took as a sedative at night. It was to stop him talking to them, the police. If he'd given it away – about that other girl – it would have strengthened the case against him, and – he might have confessed, anyway.'

'Confessed that he killed Paula?'

'Yes.'

'And do you think he did?' Doran asked.

Maggie frowned deeply.

'I've thought everything you can imagine. That he did, that he didn't, that he might have seen it happen . . . In the end I was sure he had done it, because nobody else seemed likely. He worshipped her, and she'd only have had to rebuff him when he was in one of his moods. What I couldn't understand was the way it was done, so brutal and bloody – not a bit like Guy. If it had been strangling again . . . well. There was always the other one. That's why I couldn't let him talk to the police.'

Doran put her hand on Maggie's.

'But the police know, Maggie, they found out for themselves. Mr Eastry told me. It was no secret.'

Maggie gasped. Rodney, who had not been informed

of anything about Guy's past, looked from one to the other of them.

'What did you put in the suicide note?' Doran asked.

Maggie attempted a laugh. 'I should have thought you'd have known that – you seem to know everything else. I did a scrawl in what I thought they'd take for Guy's handwriting, a sort of printing, like a child's. Something like "I can't go on, going mad". Pretty clumsy, but it must have taken them in. I tried to tell Ogle but he didn't seem to want to listen. That was later, not at the hospital after – after I found Guy in bed and I couldn't waken him. I've been through Hell. He might have died, and it would all have been my fault.'

Rodney and Doran talked in the silent language of a close marriage. No drinkies, said Doran. This is serious and she's got to stay sober. What are we going to do, for Heaven's sake?

Leave it to me, Rodney thought. I'm a priest, after all, and I've just heard a confession.

'Maggie,' he said cheerfully, 'I think I ought to take you home.'

'No! I don't want to be on my own.'

'You won't be. I'll stay with you, as long as you like. In fact you can put me up, if you feel like it. Doran won't mind, will you?'

Doran did mind, because they were so happy together this evening in the knowledge of freedom from their unwanted lodger. But it was something Rodney must do, for his own good as well as Maggie's. He would talk to her and make her feel better: Rodney always did make people feel better. She agreed that it was a very good idea, especially as she had things to get on with, like working on some objects she'd brought home from Eastgate.

Rodney murmured at the door, 'I'll ring you if I'm staying. And I'll get the bus back from Barminster in the morning. You won't say anything to the police, will you? I shouldn't.'

It had been in Doran's mind to talk to Sam.

'No, all right. I know what you mean – I ought to stay out of things, at this stage, or I'll mess something up.'

'Good girl.'

They kissed. It would have been a prolonged kiss, in other circumstances. The relief of stress is a potent aphrodisiac.

As Doran stacked the dishwasher, rejoicing in the knowledge that it was nearly the last time she would wash up after Euan, she reflected how unlike real-life crime was to the fictional kind. In a whodunit, the forged suicide note would have been analysed and recognized at once for what it was. A psychological analysis of Guy's character and criminal potential would have been on file. Ogle would have listened to Maggie's pathetic attempt to admit her cover-up. In a higher league, Poirot would have reasoned it all out by his little grey cells, and had everybody concerned breathlessly listening to his exposition of the crime. Dr Thorndyke would have got it by majestic forensic know-how. Peter Wimsey would have brought charm, erudition and wealth to bear on what must be essentially a very simple problem. Miss Marple would have quietly solved the whole thing long ago.

In the nursery was peace. No sinister Cherub on the wall, the little people of Lewis Carroll going about their quaint business in their glass case: new and old toys were neatly stacked in a painted box, Kit's colourful splodges of paint, his Young Masterpieces, had been brought home from play-school and pinned up on a cork board. Everything was unnaturally tidy, though that would change as soon as he got up tomorrow.

The very picture of angel-infancy, he was in bed, on the verge of sleep, Doran knew by the blink of eyelids that were trying to stay up. *Violets dim, but sweeter than the lids of Juno's eyes* . . . She would never have his curls cut, let them riot.

Gwenllian was sitting on the rocking horse, side-saddle, moving it gently to and fro as she sang. It was 'her' song, the song about Gwen that fascinated Kit: she had told him it was all true, she had been invited to a romantic castle by a courtly stranger. Tonight she sang it in English.

'*The lamps ahead invite you*
With pleasures to delight you:
Then homeward let them light you –
Venture, venture, venture, Gwen.'

'*Mentra,*' Kit murmured.

'That's right, love, you're learning Welsh quick. *Mentra* is the word for venture.'

The lids had fallen now. The double lashes were gold-tipped. Unfair, on a boy. But lovely.

'I'll stay with him for a while,' Gwenllian said.

'That's nice. Oh, news.' Doran told her about Euan's transfer and impending removal from Bell House. 'He's next door now, packing.'

Gwenllian nodded, still rocking, one jewelled hand twined in the horse's mane.

Doran left her, and went to the little room which she had turned into a place for storing small stock on its way to the shop, and for working on things that didn't need to go to their invaluable restorer. Tonight she would work on Dorothea.

Dorothea was a small Parian figure, from around the late 1840s, a long-haired girl in boy's clothes, resting on a journey, her little bundle of possessions at her bare feet, her shoes discarded. She was a character in *Don Quixote*, and had been modelled by a man called John Bell. His name was on the base, and the Minton mark. Doran thought of her as Dick Whittington, and half contemplated keeping her when she was cleaned up.

Meanwhile, Dorothea-Dick was coated with nasty, gungey gilt paint, applied long ago by somebody with a generous hand. It was extremely difficult to remove, but the work was rewarding and absorbing. Doran switched on her cassette player. It obliged with Elgar's *Theme and Six Diversions*, a pensive romantic piece. Elgar had written: 'A stream of music flowed through our house and the shop, and I was all the time bathing in it.'

Would Kit experience anything like that? Would the stream of antiques that flowed through Bell House get into his blood, and turn him into a dealer? Would he become an artist? Or would he follow Rodney into the Church? If so, what would the Church be like when he grew up?

Doran's speculations on her son's future were interrupted by the telephone bell. 'Blast,' she said, and went to answer it on the bedroom extension.

It was Euan. 'Could you come over for a minute? I'm in a bit of a muddle and I need some help. Sorry to bother you.'

'All right. I'll be there.'

Sorry to bother you, big deal. There hadn't been much sorrow or any apologies up to now. But it was his last night, she could spare him a few minutes in gratitude.

The evening air struck surprisingly cold. The great palette of the sky held none of the slashes of gold and rose which had been painted across it every evening since the storm. The fine summer weather was giving way to the customary grey warm nullity of August.

Against it, the ivory paintwork covering the stucco of Magnolia House had lost its fresh bandbox look, and seemed almost dirty. The tulip tree looked as though it could never have held exotic waxy white blossoms. The grass beneath it was ragged, overgrown, because Euan had not been mowing it. He had not responded to Doran's suggestion that Ozzy should do it for him.

Odd, that grief should prevent a tidy man from maintaining his garden. Doran reflected that if – an unthinkable if – she should be bereaved, she would at least see that her home was kept up in a sightly fashion. Partly for the sake of whoever had left her alone in it.

But there was something odd about Euan's grief. It had got no better, if that was the word, since he had been living at Bell House, and no worse. It was constant, the symptoms predictable. Almost as though he were behaving to a formula.

The ornate, late Gothic porch of the house was only a few steps away, but Doran's feet were curiously reluctant to approach it. She looked back towards her own front door, through the row of silver birches which divided the gardens. In Magnolia House only one window was lighted, the window of the front bedroom.

She made herself walk forward.

'It's these suits.' He was in what had been the marital bedroom, a plushy place far more female than male, very pink and frilly and flowery but in immaculate taste. Very Paula.

'I have to wear them for my sort of job,' he explained, 'but I've never folded them and I simply don't know how.'

'Obviously.' The bed, which was the sort divided into two neat halves, was covered with the separate parts of three-piece wholes – jackets, trousers, waistcoats – some of them clumsily halved with the sleeves together or crumpled up into ungainly lumps.

'Paula used to do all that sort of thing,' he said, 'if I had to go anywhere. Now I just can't cope.'

'So I see. But couldn't the removal packers do it for you? I haven't moved for years and years, thankfully, but I seem to remember that they just transported clothes on hangers or something. I should leave them if I were you.'

'I couldn't trust them. They're my best suits, you see. They cost a bomb. No, they need a woman's hand. Could you, please, Doran?'

Resignedly she began on the first trio that came to hand, grateful that Rodney's taste ran to the casual. As she straightened, folded and assembled, Euan opened a big suitcase filled with sheets of tissue paper.

'She was so thorough,' he said wistfully. 'I know she put tissue between every garment.' He was standing watching, his mouth turned down, looking something like one of those immobile figures at each corner of the catafalque at a royal lying-in-state. Of course, he too was mourning.

The bed had over it curtains in light and dark pink satin, gathered and hung like a tent. Euan saw her glance at the stylish swag, mistaking her look for admiration, which it was not. Napoleon, not a favourite of hers, had favoured such draperies.

'She – Paula – made it herself,' he said. 'And the chair covers to match.' They gleamed in the light from the swan-necked bedside lamps. So did the shining stripes of the curtains, not yet drawn.

'Ah.' Not a lot to be said, that hadn't already been said – to Paula.

'And pretty well every other bloody thing in the house, sod her, the clever-clever bitch,' continued Euan in such an ordinary conversational tone that Doran disbelieved in what she was hearing.

'And that goes for you, too,' he added, coming a step nearer.

She straightened up, moving away from him, to the far side of the bed.

'Euan?'

'You were laughing at me tonight, weren't you – you

and that poncy egg-head husband of yours. I heard you, and those bloody silly songs. You think I'm just a poor fool compared with your lot, don't you?'

'No, of course not. I – '

'So did she, so did Perfect Paula. That was what you used to call her, didn't you? Oh, I knew, giggling with people in corners. She was cleverer than you, though, for all your mouldy antiques and your books and your poof of a partner and that old witch of a mother of his. I was very proud of Paula, once. It only wore off when I found she thought I was a worm. Oh yes, she did. She used to show off for both of us, because there was nothing she could show off about me. They wouldn't even give me a part in that crap, that opera. So she did it all, and I went after her bleating like a little lamb about how I adored her. Well, I had once, so it became second nature, didn't it?'

Horrible how people's familiar faces changed when they were white-hot with stored rage and madness. He was nearer now. There was foam, or something, at the corners of his lips. The colourless, rather dreary person who had been her next-door neighbour and lodger had turned into this coarse shouting lunatic.

'You don't mean all that,' Doran managed to whisper through dry lips.

'Don't I, you stupid cow? Paula unmanned me – know what I mean? When she realized that, she despised me even more than she had. She tried the others out, did you know? Oh, nothing heavy, just a bit here and there. She was a teaser, she enjoyed that. She liked working men up . . .'

'Who, for instance?' Better to keep him talking.

'Sexy Rupert, of course, and that moron of a boy who went for me after Max had bawled her out over that dress. Did you hear what he called me?'

'Yes – I think we all did.'

He was advancing nearer, round the bed.

'Have your police friends told you what I said I was doing that night – the night she's supposed to have run off?'

'No.' That was true enough. 'It's none of my business.' She hoped her voice wasn't shaking, as her knees were.

'I don't believe you. But I'll tell you what really happened.'

'Do.' Doran tried to sound casually interested, instead of terrified.

'We had a scene in the car, coming back from the rehearsal. She'd been off in the woods for half an hour with Rupert. I thought of driving away and leaving her to get home the best way she could – then I found I was too steamed up for that. I wanted to see her, I had to see her. But somehow I couldn't get it out, she niggled and answered back and I stopped trying.

'When we got home I wanted to go to bed. With her. I thought that would solve something. But she went into her sewing room and started snipping the sequins off that bloody dress. I kept asking her to stop, but she wouldn't, just snip, snip, snip. Then she put the thing on and started posing in front of the long mirror. She started on about the night Max had criticized the dress. She'd never been so insulted, she said.

'And it was all my fault, she said, I could have stopped it, if I'd been a man, but I wasn't. She'd never said such things to me – even she. I could have killed her. I made up my mind I would kill her.

'She made it easy for me. She said she'd left her costume hat at the school and she was going to drive back and fetch it, and alter it, too. I said, "All right, I'll come with you." And I did. We went back to Elvesham, and she noticed nothing, just sang some idiotic song from that piece. That opera.'

Doran wondered desperately what Gilbert and Sullivan would have said, and whether those innocent men could have dreamed up such a situation.

'I knew what I was going to do when we got to Elvesham, though I didn't know how, or what it was going to be like. I just thought about hitting her.'

Doran began to fold a jacket with automatic neatness, to give him something to look aside at. But his eyes were on her face, avidly watching her reaction.

'It didn't quite work out as I'd meant when we got to Elvesham. She knew, by then. She was frightened, and she wasn't singing any more. When I stopped the car she almost fell out, and started running. I hadn't expected that and it took me quite a bit of time to catch up with her.'

Of course, that was when Kate Lidell had seen Paula's flying figure.

'But I did, just as she got up to the school. I grabbed her, and she screamed a lot, but there was nobody about. I kept hitting her until she stopped screaming. Then I dragged her into that scruffy garden. I knew what I was doing, yet I didn't – if you can understand that.'

'Oh, I can, Euan – it's known as the John Jasper Syndrome. The only clue Dickens left to *The Mystery of Edwin Drood* was – '

'Shut up. I saw that chopper of Turner's and hit her over the head with it. She yelled and passed out, at least I think she did. I don't remember what I thought then, except that it seemed a pity to waste the chance of having a chopper in my hand. So I hit her across the neck. I didn't know Turner had sharpened it. It gave me a shock, I can tell you, all that blood. I've never seen so much blood . . .

'Sit down, you've gone green. It doesn't suit you.' He pushed her into a sitting position on the bed, on the side away from the telephone.

'Then I hung about, sort of letting her drain. It

seemed to take hours. There was a pile of garden sacks in the shed, so I bundled her up in them and carried her into the school. The door was locked, but I'd noticed the other one. The one you got in by.'

'That was clever of you.' Flatter them. Murderers like it.

Euan leaned over and struck her across the face. 'I told you to shut up, didn't I? That carved box of yours was up there on the stage, so I pushed her into it. Thought I'd buy myself a bit of time before they found her. Then I tidied up in the garden and went home by the back road and got myself a drink. Several drinks. Alone. In my own house. Nobody to tell me not to. No yak-yak, no superior smirk. That was what I'd wanted. Next day I just went back to being the devoted husband. Easy. Didn't I do it well?'

It was very hard to keep talking, when all one's instincts were to push past him to the window and hammer on it and scream, but she forced out words.

'Euan, why didn't you just leave her? You could have got a divorce.'

People had said that about Crippen.

'She wouldn't have let me. And how'd I have lived? She had all the money. Now it's mine. I drew it out of the bank today – well, a lot of it.'

'But – '

'They couldn't stop me. The account was in our joint names, right? I'm going away tonight. Not where I told you, that was all a front. No, I'm going right away, somewhere they won't look for me. But first I'm going to kill you.'

'Oh, don't . . . Euan, don't! Why?'

'First because it'll be a pleasure, and second because if I don't you'll talk, and give me less time to get away. Just the car and my clothes, that's all I'm taking, I don't care about the bloody house and her fiddling needlework and her Swedish kitchen or whatever it is. I never did like you, Doran.'

He had opened a drawer behind him, and now held a pair of tights, strung like a cord between his hands. Doran screamed, once, and tried to remember what she had seen of unarmed combat on television, as he grasped her shoulders.

'Oh, I wouldn't do that, if I were you,' said a soft voice from the door. Gwenllian strolled into the room. She was carrying Doran's drawing room poker, a heavy affair of eighteenth-century iron. Euan's hands dropped away from Doran's neck.

Gwenllian smiled at him.

'I can use this, you know, I'm stronger than I look. You have a very soft skull, I should say. We'll see, shall we?'

As she advanced Euan let out a stream of obscene words, a flood of disconnected raving, and rushed towards the door. Gwenllian stood aside politely for him, the poker raised. They heard him clatter down the stairs and slam the front door. A car started into life. Gwenllian watched from the window with calm interest.

'There now, he's off,' she observed.

'He forgot his suitcase,' said Doran, and collapsed.

14

Curtain

Gwenllian's little hired car stood at the gate of Bell House, its driver beside it, wearing a very neat indigo dress patterned with a riot of tropical flowers the size of cabbages.

'But why won't you stay longer?' Doran, Rodney and Kit were a farewell party. 'We need you, it's not just the little detail that you saved Doran's life,' said Rodney.

'Oah, it was nothing. I knew where she'd gone, and I'd already sensed that your mourning widower was up to no good. So I followed, and took the precaution of listening outside the door – for witness's evidence, you see. The police would believe the two of us.'

'Oh, they did, they did, and acted on it. Very sharp of them to snap him up before he'd got even halfway to the airport. I shall never criticize the police again.'

'Even Ogle,' added Doran.

'Even Ogle. Euan may get Broadmoor if he's lucky, but I doubt it. Personally, I shan't mind what he gets.' Rodney put his arm round Doran. '*From the dungeon to the block, from the scaffold to the grave*, is what he'd be in for if we were back in the days of good old Horrible Henry, and a good thing too. God forgive me for saying so.'

'That's very true,' said Gwenllian. 'Now it will take me all of an hour to get to Hywel's, what with all the traffic there is, and then I will be starting on my coach tour of Beautiful Scotland.'

'Will you come back?' Kit asked, holding on to her hand.

'I will come back and back, till you're tired of seeing me.'

'Tell me some more stories?'

'You learn to read, *bach*, and you can tell me stories. Goodbye now.' She kissed them all, a butterfly's touch in a cloud of fragrance.

Doran said, 'Thank you again, Gwenllian. Thank you so much.'

'Don't thank me. I only came to help.' She turned the key in the ignition.

'I believe she *did* come to help. She was sent.'

'I've always believed in divine Sendings,' Rodney said, very seriously. '*And* in fairies. Kit didn't cry, you note, as he did when Tiggy left.' He could mention her name now without even an extra heartbeat.

'No. They've got *Tŵm Sion Catti* in the library children's section, in paperback – I shall get it. Rodney, hasn't everything changed? The police know Guy's innocent now, and Maggie's happy, and Ruth's getting better, and . . . and it's all over.' She hadn't mentioned another thing that they both knew was over.

'You know,' she went on, 'there's only one thing I regret – that there's never going to be a *Yeomen*.'

'Poor old St Leonard's will regret that, too, when it finally falls down. I wonder if . . .'

Doran caught his thought instantly.

'. . . if we could put the cast together again, when all this has died down – ask Edwin Dutton if he'd let us use the church hall here, and do a *real* production – with no murder interruptions or anything like that? I miss that music, and the fun there could have been. Shall we try?'

'We will. St Leonard's needs us.' And how I should

like to be Jack Point again, he thought, surprised at himself.

Doran kissed him. 'I kept the costume,' she said.